4.4

For P

With all good wishes

John W. Daniel

Red Clay and Brunswick Stew

RED CLAY AND BRUNSWICK STEW

John W. Daniel

Copyright ©2021 by John W. Daniel

All rights reserved

ISBN-13: 979-8577886110

To Sharon

My wife, editor, and best friend

CONTENTS

A Small Confusion (1961)   1

Lester (1964)   9

Island Fog (1966)   19

Old Women (1968)   29

Time to Hang it Up (1970)   43

Just Passing Through (1973)   57

Course of Distinction (1982)   69

Ellie and Bus (1986)   82

Once in a Great While (1993)   97

Railroad Man (1971-2000)   112

Cindy's Poem (2004)   136

The Prodigal (2005)   152

The Good Doctor (2009)   165

Welcome to the Neighborhood (2013)   178

Harvey's Coup (2016)   189

The March (2020)   204

AUTHOR'S NOTE

Chockoyotte (pronounced "choc-yot" with an emphasis on the first syllable) is believed to be a Tuscarora Indian word. Though its meaning is no longer known, the word shows up regularly in North Carolina's Halifax County. Chockoyotte Street, Chockoyotte Park, and Chockoyotte Baptist Church are all located in the small city of Roanoke Rapids. Chockoyotte Creek flows past the nearby town of Weldon into the Roanoke River. Chockoyotte Country Club, an upscale eighteen-hole golf course, abuts the southwestern edge of Weldon.

In this collection of short stories, the town Chockoyotte is a fictionalized version of Weldon. Both sets of my grandparents lived in Weldon, my parents grew up there, and I often visited there when I was a boy. Occasionally I got to play golf at Chockoyotte Country Club, which at the time had only nine holes. The ninth hole in those days was exactly as Moses Bibby described it in "Course of Distinction."

A SMALL CONFUSION (1961)

My father says we got some good niggers in this town and we got some bad ones too, and I reckon that's a fact. For instance, a good nigger would be Slim Bazemore that works the case packer at the Coca Cola plant—handles a job would take two white men to work. Slim wouldn't think about being uppity to white folks, anymore than he'd think about being shiftless and letting welfare support him because he doesn't have a white collar job. Slim knows where he belongs and he's happy there.

Like Granger Tatum, another good darkie, the one that goes on most of the hunts with the men around here, cooks for 'em, skins the kill. Why, Granger is happy as a clam so long as you give him a bottle of wine and some of the meat to take home. And then there's Roosevelt and Nettie Whitley that been working for my folks as long as I can remember, always smiling and asking about my school work and whether I plan to be a fine lawyer like my father when I grow up. I told 'em they didn't have to call me Master Doug, that just plain Doug is fine with me—but I didn't insist because they got kind of shy and ducked their heads, and I didn't want to hurt their feelings.

On the other side of the ledger, on the debit side, you got niggers like Selma Newsome that used to teach over at Ralph Bunche High School until she got arrested in one of those demonstrations where they all sit down in the street and block traffic. Father said our niggers, the good ones, got to be protected from people like Selma. Imagine what would happen if she stirred 'em up and got a group to sit down on Washington Avenue trying to stop our traffic—why, in five minutes flat you'd have to scrape 'em off the pavement with a putty knife. So Selma doesn't teach at Ralph Bunche any more. Father's on the school board here and he's just as concerned about what the colored kids are taught as he is us.

Then there's Clivie Dillard and his gang of mean-looking blacks that stroll around downtown like they dare you to look at 'em straight, like if you even think "pickaninny," they'd just as soon jerk out a switchblade or a razor and come at you with it. Clivie is a bad one all right. One day he walked right into Pitman's Drug Store and ordered a Pepsi, which is OK by me, but he didn't take the Pepsi and leave like most of our colored folks would've done. No, he spotted Miss Dolly Farnesworth, all two hundred pounds of her, sitting at the counter eating that banana split she comes in for every afternoon from her beauty shop across the street. And he saunters up behind her and leans down and says he sure is tired, yes ma'am. Miss Dolly huddles down over her banana split shivering from that nigger breath hot on her neck, and Clivie says he sure could use that stool beside her to rest his bones on, and sits down right next to Miss Dolly and starts sipping his Pepsi, making slurping noises with his straw. When she finally turns around and looks at him, Clivie has his face right up next to hers and he says "Boo," barely loud enough for Charmaine Gilliam behind the counter to hear him, but Miss Dolly jumps out of her seat and flies out the door like she was shot from a cannon. She didn't stop till she got to the police station and signed a warrant for Clivie's arrest, and Clivie back at the drug store laughing like he's going to bust a gut, Charmaine said.

Clivie got sixty days in jail for it. Of course, he didn't hurt Miss Dolly, but that ain't the point of it. Like Father said, a nigger can't be allowed to show disrespect for a white woman, even if she has had to close down her shop twice because of goings-on in the back room, if you know what I mean. If Clivie had got away with that, the next thing you know he and his bunch would be doing the same thing to the respectable white women of the town. Give 'em an inch and they'll take a mile, Father says.

Then there's Silas Jackman who's always hanging around downtown bumming change to buy a pint of wine and bragging to anybody'll listen about how he's descended from Colonel Patterson whose statue is between the high school and Cedarwood Cemetery. I never thought Silas was exactly a bad nigger, though he's got his faults all right. For a long time I just wasn't sure where Silas belonged, whether he was a bad nigger that had his good points or a good nigger with bad points. It was downright confusing, because I knew he's got to be one or the other—there's just no getting around it.

Anyway, Silas claims his grandmother was one of the colonel's slave girls and his grandfather was the colonel himself, and whenever he gets high on wine, he usually goes and sits under that statue and looks up at it with dreamy eyes like he's worshiping it. Or if he gets real drunk, he heads for Miss Annie Laurie Patterson's house, like he did last night. Miss Annie Laurie is the great niece of the colonel and her family gave most of the money for his statue to be built in the first place. One time she came to Father to see if anything could be done about Silas, have him sent away to an insane asylum or have Mr. Buck Condor the police chief lock him up for good or something, because he was always disgracing her family name. Well, last night, Mr. Buck caught Silas outside Miss Annie Laurie's bedroom window, and I guess he was some kind of mad, because he didn't take Silas to jail for the night like he usually does when he's drunk. He just drove him down to the Chalk 'N Cue where Ned Copeland and his buddies were and turned Silas over. Ned drives in the stock car races around here and mostly he wins. Everybody knows Ned Copeland, and we all admire him a lot.

Well, last night was Friday, the night me and Merle Haverling get to stay out late. So after we took in the early picture show down at the Silver Screen we decided to stop by the Chalk 'N Cue and play the pinball machine in the back before going home. We were playing and listening to Ned and the guys talking up front about the race coming up next week in

Martinsville when all of a sudden Silas stumbled in the door ahead of Mr. Buck, and the eyes lit up all around like the lights on that pinball machine when you break a thousand and free games start ringing up BING, BING, BING, and you still got one ball left and you know the fun is just getting ready to start. Silas noticed it too, groggy as he was, because he tried to duck back out the door. But Mr. Buck swung him back inside and handed him to Ned, almost gentle, like he was giving Ned a present and didn't want to jostle it around too much because it might break before he got a chance to use it good. Then Mr. Buck yawned and said he was going back to his office to finish the paperwork he'd started before Miss Annie Laurie telephoned him and he sure hoped he wouldn't be bothered again by any more nigger peeping Toms.

All the guys laughed and when Mr. Buck was gone they looked at each other, and then without saying a word, like they'd agreed on it beforehand, they drug Silas out in the alley where two or three of them held him while Ned slapped his face a few times to sober him up good. Silas kind of lay slumped in their arms whining and moaning, his eyes rolled back in their sockets like they are when he's looking up at that statue of Colonel Patterson. Then Ned said since Silas liked to be around white people so much maybe he'd like to be white himself because Miss Annie Laurie Patterson would never invite a nigger in her bedroom but all a white man would have to do was tap on the glass and she'd drag him over the sill herself. Silas just shook his head and his face screwed up and he started saying, "No suh, no suh," over and over, adding a "Please" every now and then like you unstick a record and it gets right back stuck again.

Then Ned said how about a little paint and feather job, and directly Bull Moose Meechum ran down the alley toward the hotel and Shag Draper took off in the other direction. After a while Bull Moose came back with an armful of pillows and started slitting them open with his pocket knife. Then the rest of the guys began pulling off Silas' clothes with Silas pleading "No suh" and "Please" until before he knew what was happening he was squatting down stripped naked, his hands and arms moving up his legs like he was trying to pull on a pair of pants that weren't there, and all of us laughing to beat the band. Finally when Silas realized he didn't have anything but skin to pull at, he just sat down on the ground in a heap, his eyes rolled back in his head further than ever, whimpering.

After a minute or two Shag came back with two cans of white paint and pried the lids off. When he started pouring, Silas went to yelling and squirming, like somebody was trying to kill him. Ned jerked him up and slapped him across the face while Shag kept on pouring, drenching Silas' head first, then sloshing the paint on his chest and back, letting it run down his legs. Every time Silas would start to let out a yell Ned would slap him across the face good and solid with the back of his hand and Silas would go back to whimpering.

When the paint cans were empty, all the guys started breaking the pillows on him and feathers were flying every which a way. Silas wasn't even squirming now, so it didn't take long. When the feathers were all stuck on good, Ned let go and Silas slumped back on the ground white as snow all over, looking like a big white bird, and everybody hollered and doubled up laughing.

We went on laughing and pounding each other on the back for a long time, pointing our fingers at the sight, until finally Ned said it was time to shoot some more pool. But before he left, Ned walked over and slapped Silas two or three more times across the mouth for good measure and told him never to come near any white woman again, even if it was one like Miss Annie Laurie that was nearbout forty years old.

Well, I enjoyed it. It was a good show, better than the Roy Rogers movie me and Merle saw at the Silver Screen before going to the Chalk 'N Cue. I enjoyed it all the way home, except maybe the slapping part. I was sorry Ned slapped Silas that last time, but besides that it was a good joke, and I still enjoyed it after I went to bed, giggling to myself about Silas laying on the ground like an overgrown white chicken.

Then my mind started playing a trick on me. Out of a clear sky it started saying "OK Silas you can get up now. Brush yourself off and go on home. The joke's over." But for some reason I couldn't see him get up. It was like when you go to bed and you play a game with your mind, like baseball maybe and you decide you want to hit a home run and the pitcher throws one right where you want it but you swing under it or over it every time. If you're asleep, you might connect, but when you're still awake and try to think the ball over the fence, if you're really concentrating as hard as you can, you can't hit that ball to save your life. At least I can't. So when I tried to think Silas off the ground, he wouldn't budge. No matter how hard I tried to raise him off the ground in my mind, he wouldn't get up. He just lay there, naked and white with all those feathers stuck to him and his eyes rolled back in his head. And then I wasn't enjoying it anymore at all, seeing Silas laying there like he was dead, like he wasn't ever going to get up.

After a while I got out of bed and put on my clothes and snuck down the stairs. I got almost to the front door when Father caught me with his voice. I told him I was thirsty and was going to the kitchen for a drink of water.

Which was just as well, better in fact, because this morning Silas was downtown as usual, bumming change and talking about Colonel Patterson, like nothing had happened. I don't know how he got all that paint and feathers off so quick, but I sure was glad he did. And when I passed him on the street, he smiled at me like he does to most everybody. Right then I had an urge to go over and tell him something, say something nice to him, like you might go over and stroke an old hound that's always been faithful to you, one you treated bad at times but he forgave you. I wanted to go over and say, "Silas, you *are* a good nigger, you really *are*." But then I remembered how Roosevelt and Nettie got embarrassed when I told then it was all right to call me by my first name, so I just smiled back and passed on.

LESTER (1964)

After nudging the sweepings into a pile with his broom, Lester Brogden leaned against the door jamb to watch the rain slant across the church yard in thick, heavy sheets. It had been raining ever since daybreak, the smell of it hanging keen in the air. He breathed deeply, sucking the clean wet fragrance down into his lungs. And he listened to the rain's loud steady rhythm, as if it were a special kind of music which he alone understood, separating in his mind the two distinct tones—one made by the water splashing on the steps and the flagstone court below him, and the other, deeper and more penetrating, made by its pounding against the gravel of the horseshoe drive and the turf of the yard.

Now that the lightning and thunder had subsided, Lester liked everything about this rain—the feel of it on his skin, its scent, the sounds it made—but he especially liked the strange feeling of security it gave him. Standing at the edge of the vestibule, it was as if he had a wall of protection around him and he was completely safe, in a world where everything was clean and fresh and pure. There was no Chockoyotte, only a brief blurred segment of Washington Avenue at the end of the church grounds. Beyond this, the rain had eased out everything—even the fact that Jesse Poindexter would soon be leaving his home, and the likelihood that the white people would find some way to keep him out of their church. There was only the purifying and protecting rain, which began at the end of Lester's vision, in the dull aluminum grayness above the trees, and splashed against the steps and the flagstones or spattered on the grass-covered earth of the church yard.

Reaching out his hand and feeling the cool sharp tingling of the water, Lester let his thoughts drift slowly over pleasant things—the sawmill with its sweet turpentine smell and shrill sounds of lumber being cut, the softball game he had played yesterday in a pasture south of town, his family. For a moment his mind hovered about his family and he thought of his two daughters and how much they had grown the last couple of years, realizing how lucky he was to have this extra job on Sundays so he wouldn't have to worry about his regular job at the sawmill not providing enough money to take care of their needs. He pulled back his hand, wiped it absently on his trousers, and stared at the sycamore trees where at each gust of wind the leaves swirled inside out, their undersides spreading into a glossy white. A shiver of contentment ran up his spine.

After a while he picked up the dustpan from beside the door and began sweeping the trash into it, emptying the contents of the pan into a large pasteboard barrel. As he moved away from the door, the fresh sound of the rain lessened and was replaced by a muffled metallic drone as it pelted the roof. Thunder rumbled in the distance and Lester's hand tightened on the broom handle, then relaxed again as he continued sweeping. When he finished he put the broom and pan in the barrel which he slid into a closet, then took a mop from a bucket near the door, wrung out the water, and began swabbing the floor, humming a tune as he worked.

Before long there was the sound of a car crunching over the wet gravel on the driveway, coming to a stop in front of the church. A door slammed and a white man hurried up the steps and into the vestibule.

"Mornin', Mr. Barlow," Lester said, slipping into the servile tone that came second nature to him in the presence of most white people. "Mite early, aren't you?"

"Hello, Lester." The minister shook the rain from his umbrella and began wiping his face with a handkerchief. "The service starts at ten-thirty this morning. I meant to get in touch with you about it but ... well, no harm done I see. You should be finished in plenty of time."

"Yes, sir." Lester dipped the mop into the pail, shook it, and squeezed out the excess water with the wringer. As he started the long back and forward strokes of the mop, his eyes narrowed and a puzzled look spread over his face. He stopped mopping and shifted weight from one foot to the other. "That got somethin' to do with Jesse, Mr. Barlow?"

Though not yet middle-aged, the minister was overweight and his chin had gone flabby. "I'm afraid it does," he said in a gentle voice. "And as much as I hate to, Lester, I'm going to have to ask for your cooperation."

Lester resumed his swabbing, edging away from the minister. He was a little older than the white man and much larger; he had a big chest and muscular arms. The skin around his eyes resembled leather from a shoe that had been worn a long time.

"You'll have to lock the door when the service begins," the minister said, his voice still soft and apologetic. "That's what the vestry decided last Sunday after Jesse came to the service. They decided to begin today's service early ... and to lock the door."

A sudden gust of rain sprayed the window of the vestibule and the wind whistled in the rafters of the belfry. Lester put the mop in the bucket, resting the handle against the wall, then took a cloth from his hip pocket and began dusting around the door to the inside of the church.

"Reckon I can't," he said. "Reckon you better not ask me to do that."

"Believe me, I understand your feelings," the minister said. Moving closer he laid a tentative hand on Lester's shoulder. "It's the vestry that decided this. Please understand I've had nothing to do with it. If there were any other way, I'd never ask you."

His jaw slack and his eyes dull, Lester continued to dust. Only his arm moved, slowly and perfunctorily, back and forth over the door. There was a long muffled rumble of thunder, beginning low, rising, then falling away into the drone of the rain.

"It's not me, Lester," the minister said, gripping the black man's shoulder. "It's the vestry. You can understand that. And ... well ... they are not simply asking. They are telling. They want you to be the one to keep Jesse away." He removed his hand to wipe perspiration from his face.

Lester looked dully at the wood, his arm continuing the dusting motion. "Why me, Mr. Barlow?" he asked, his voice a mixture of pleading and perplexity.

The minister seemed not to hear the question. "Believe me, I understand. You're in the same position I'm in. I have a wife and children and so do you. If it wasn't for my family I'd never be a party to this." He drew closer and again placed his hand on Lester's shoulder. "Lester," he said. "Lester ... I'm an integrationist."

"Sir?" A gust of wind sprayed the window and rattled the panes. The sound of the rain grew louder for a moment, then settled back into its rhythmic pounding.

"Why ... why, don't you know what an integrationist is?"

"No sir," Lester lied and began dusting the table by the door where a stack of pamphlets lay. The hand slipped from his shoulder.

"Well, never mind. The point is I want Jesse to be here for our services. I truly do. But can you imagine what would happen if my parishioners heard me saying that? In another ten or fifteen years maybe. But not now." He paused. "A minister can't get too far ahead of his flock, you know."

Lester gazed at the stack of pamphlets. "Reckon I can't do it, Mr. Barlow."

The minister shook his head sadly. "You have to do it, Lester."

"What you mean?"

"I mean Fletcher Stephenson. He's the presiding officer of the vestry. *He* wants you to do it."

The crunching of gravel sounded above the rain as a car pulled up in front of the church. The minister took a step toward the inner door. "There's no other way. We both have to participate—as unjust as our participation might be."

Lester looked at the rain beyond the open door and saw lightning snake across the sky. Turning away he lifted the religious pamphlets and dusted under them, then put them back on the table. A peal of thunder reverberated through the vestibule.

"I'm sorry," the minister said, his voice trembling, "but either you lock that door when the service begins or … or I'm afraid you won't have a job tomorrow. Neither here nor at the sawmill." Then he moved through the door and into the church proper before the first members of the congregation arrived.

Standing in his usual position beside the bell rope, Lester barely noticed the white people as they filed through the vestibule, shaking raindrops from their umbrellas and removing their galoshes. His mind lay more with the minister, hoping the man didn't really mean everything he'd said, hoping the part about his livelihood was a threat and nothing more. Outside, the rain had increased and every few moments lightning flared across the sky, followed by heavy bursts of thunder.

Presently a jovial-looking man and his family came through the door and began taking off their raincoats, the woman shaking her umbrella and setting it in a corner. After she nudged the two children through the door and into the church, the man walked over to Lester.

"You like workin' at the sawmill?" he asked, the tone of his words pleasant, but there was a distinct undertone in his voice.

Lester looked vaguely past the man's shoulder, the skin around his eyes flinching, his jaw slack. "Yes, sir."

The man nodded. "I like having you work for me too. It's hard to find a man as dependable as you nowadays." He placed a hand lightly on Lester's arm. "But it's _not_ impossible." He looked knowingly at Lester and smiled. "Just 'splain that to Jesse. Tell him how your future depends on how reasonable he decides to be." He turned and walked toward the interior of the church. Before he got there he swung around. "Better tend to that door now. Ain't nobody else coming to the service this mornin'."

Lester wanted to sit down but there was no chair, so he walked to the outside door and let the breeze cool his face. Lightning flashed and he drew back a little just as thunder exploded, trailing off into a long irregular rumbling. He took the cloth from his back pocket and wiped sweat from his face, cursing Jesse Poindexter under his breath for putting him in such a senseless predicament.

Lester understood this: Aside from owning the sawmill, Fletcher Stephenson was a member of the Ku Klux Klan and definitely not a man to truck with. Yet Jesse Poindexter had managed to get the best of him without even knowing it because Jesse wouldn't let Stephenson or any other white man bother him any more than he would a flea. He was too old; all anybody could do to him would be to take his life away, and he was ready to give that up anyhow. Jesse had outlived his wife and most of his children and had decided that since he was born a certain denomination he ought to die a member of the same one, and if the only church of that denomination this side of Richmond was white, the old mule was bound and determined to attend that one. Jesse's mind had grown so feeble he didn't care about consequences anymore. Fletcher Stephenson knew that. He also knew that other than killing Jesse there wasn't anything could be done about him except treat another black man in the fashion he wished he could treat Jesse. Somehow that would make it right; a black man would be cowed and Jesse wouldn't show up at the church again, the result being the same as if Jesse had been scared off first hand.

Lester eased back toward the congregation and gazed over their heads at the door of the sacristy where the choir would file out, where on rainy days he received the signal to ring the bell. He swung his eyes back over the congregation, pausing momentarily where Fletcher Stephenson sat with his family. Lester didn't hate the man for using him to get back at Jesse, just as he didn't hate white people in general. All his life they had been like natural hazards he simply had to abide in order to keep on surviving, like the thunder and lightning he sometimes had to put up with in order to enjoy a rain. He didn't hate the lightning. He was just afraid of it, didn't want to get too close to it because it might strike him down.

As he watched Fletcher Stephenson, Lester saw out of the corner of his eye the sacristy door open and a few choir members appear, and he turned and walked slowly to the edge of the vestibule near the window. He stood for a moment beside the bell rope, then shook his head and heaved the rope down to the floor and released it. The clang was muffled in the thunder and the beating of the rain. Lester rang the bell four more times, then tied the rope on a hook in the corner just as the organ boomed the notes of the opening hymn.

When the singing began, loud and slightly cacophonous, and the choir filed into the church, Lester went to the outside door and watched the rain fall in thick steady sheets, thumping against the tops of the cars. He noticed the headlights burning on one of the cars and made a mental note to turn them off as soon as the storm lessened. Just then he saw Jesse Poindexter amble slowly onto the church driveway, frail and bent under his umbrella.

Lester edged back into the vestibule, a wave of resentment rising in him. "Old fool," he muttered. "Serves you right for not being reasonable 'bout things." But as his hand closed around the knob, Lester found himself looking at it, trying to believe the hand wasn't connected to him but was someone else's and he was watching it do something. But he knew that was a lie; it was his hand on the knob all right. With this knowledge swirling in his mind along with terrible thoughts concerning his own and his family's welfare, he stood motionless, as if rapt in the singing of the hymn, his hand still clutching the knob.

Then suddenly he was in the rain, moving down the steps, across the flagstone courtyard, and onto the graveled drive, walking fast. When he passed Jesse, Lester spoke to him, keeping his face averted so the old man couldn't see the agitation that was there. Jesse looked up in surprise, his lips moving on the beginning of a greeting. Then he shook his head and continued on toward the church, reaching the open door just as the congregation began proclaiming the Amen.

When he came to the pavement of Washington Avenue, Lester turned south, toward his home, and broke into a run, the rain pelting his face and saturating his clothes. The fact that lightning flashed around him, followed almost immediately by the crashing and rumbling of thunder, didn't even register in his mind.

ISLAND FOG (1966)

From where she stood at the clothesline, Amy Copeland could barely see the sagging back porch and the tin roof that sloped down over it. Beyond the house the fog hid everything—the dirt road, the mailbox, even the willow tree in the side yard. Visibility was so poor she felt a sudden rush of anxiety about her mother and little brother, who had left shortly after dawn to spend the day with Aunt Sally in Scotland Neck, a short drive from Caledonia Prison.

Oh, they'll be fine, Amy decided as she pinned a wet towel to the line. God looks after saints and the innocent, and goodness knows Mama's a saint to put up with that man. She reached into the clothes basket for another item, a flannel shirt that belonged to her father. She resisted an impulse to spit on it as she hung it up.

As she pinned one of her nursing bras to the line, Amy thought of Troy Tate, imagining the young man was standing there in the fog admiring her breasts, still swollen with milk. As if for his benefit, she arched her back and thrust out her chest, pleased she had regained her figure so soon after childbirth. She could almost feel Troy's hands, taste his kisses.

"Free at last!" she cried, knowing the two of them would have the place to themselves until tomorrow afternoon at the earliest. She laughed as her voice came echoing back across the yard.

After hanging up the clothes, Amy scampered back to the house, sidestepping a ceramic statue of a bearded holy man doing battle with Satan, then dancing past a bullet-riddled tree stump surrounded by tin cans and broken glass. The thought that her father would soon be using that stump again for target practice, as unpleasant as it was, failed to dampen her spirits.

She bounded up the sagging steps and hurried across the porch. The screen door slammed behind her, the noise echoing like the sound of her father's deer rifle. The fog whirled for a moment around the steps, then settled into a white stillness.

Half an hour later Amy was on her way to Chockoyotte, walking fast, her baby cradled against her neck. The fog was so thick she could hardly distinguish the road from the fields on either side. To her left a few random corn stalks poked through the whiteness, but to her right all signs of the cotton field and the river had disappeared.

"Whole island looks like a big eraser swept over it, Hannah," she said to her daughter. "Left a bunch of chalk dust on everything."

The simile reminded Amy of English class, which

was where she had been when she finally decided what to do about the fact that she was pregnant. After the bell rang, she walked with Troy to his locker and told him the news.

"You don't have to look so glum," she said. "It's not the end of the world."

"Might as well be. Soon as your dad finds out, I'm dead meat."

"He's not going to find out."

"He's got to eventually."

Amy shook her head. "I'm not going to tell him or anybody else who the father is."

"Won't it be obvious?"

"Not if we stop seeing each other now while nobody's the wiser. Right now you're the only one who knows. I should be able to keep it a secret until after you graduate. People will start talking this summer, I guess, but you can tell them we were just friends. They won't have any reason not to believe you."

"It's your dad who scares the shit out of me."

"He won't be a problem."

"How can you be so sure?"

"He doesn't know you from Adam. And I plan to keep it that way."

Troy gave her a quizzical look. "Why are you doing this, Amy?"

Though she hadn't told him everything, what she said to him now was the absolute truth. "If we end up getting married someday, I'd like it to be because you want to, not because you have to."

A look of relief spread over the young man's face.

"You're really going to take all the heat yourself?"

Amy nodded. "You're a free man, Troy Tate. I won't stand between you and your future."

"You're incredible, Amy ... one in a million."

"Finish high school and then do whatever you want—go to college, join the army, anything that suits your fancy. If along the way you decide you want me and the little one to be part of your life ... well, you'll know where to find us."

"What'll you do ... after you have the baby, I mean?"

"I don't know. I'd like to finish high school and go to college, but that's probably out of the question now. Are you still going to work at your dad's store this summer?"

"Far as I know."

"Mind if I stop by and see you sometime? I don't want us to lose touch. We'll just have to be, you know, discreet."

"Sure, I understand. Yeah, stop by anytime. Listen, Amy, I gotta go. I'm late for history class."

That was the last real conversation she'd had with Troy. Once school was out and she could no longer hide her pregnancy, things had gotten so crazy—her mother's almost constant barrage of questions concerning the baby's paternity, her father's third arrest for poaching, Hannah's birth—that she hadn't really had a chance to see him.

Three staccato shrieks rose from somewhere near the river, giving Amy a start and causing her daughter to squirm.

"That's just a crow," she crooned and shifted the

baby higher on her shoulder. "They're mean to other birds, but they don't mess with folks, even little ones like you."

Again she thought of Troy, who would be at the Western Auto by now waiting on customers. She would purchase something from him—a fishing lure for her brother's birthday or maybe a package of mousetraps—and then, since Mr. Tate or a customer would probably be within earshot, slip Troy the note.

A soft padding sound interrupted Amy's thoughts, and she swung around, staring into the whiteness. After a moment her face relaxed, the corners of her mouth lifting in a smile.

"Who you think you're fooling back there, Elvis?" She waited for the hound to materialize out of the mist. "Yeah, I see you now." She watched the lean head push through the fog. "Had no intention of letting us slip away, did you?"

The dog, mottled with splotches of brown over white, flopped down on his haunches and began to pant, his head moving up and down in rhythm with his lolling tongue. Then, as though she just remembered it belonged there, a harsh look came over Amy's face. "I don't want any more company this morning," she said, keeping her voice low so it wouldn't disturb her daughter. "Go back to the house."

The dog stayed put, his tail slapping the road.

"It'll look silly," she went on, her voice harsher. "An old hound traipsing along behind like we're hillbillies. Go on, git." She gave the dog a final leer and turned away.

When she realized she was still being followed,

Amy whirled around. "Just like a male," she said, glaring at the hound. "Do any way you please and never mind me. I've got rights too, you know. I've got a right to decide who'll leave me alone and ..." She hesitated, as though not wholly confident of her pronouncement. "And who'll take an interest."

After a moment her expression softened, and she leaned down and patted the dog's head. "Soon as we get to the gut then, you go back to the house. I mean it." She started walking again, the hound following gingerly at her heels.

A few minutes later the trio entered a thick bank of fog where the road was scarcely visible. Slowing her pace, Amy squinted into the haze as if trying to locate a familiar object. A crow shrieked from somewhere in the whiteness and was answered by another, the sounds resonating in the stillness.

"If I didn't know different," she said to her two companions, glad for the moment at least to have the dog nearby, "I'd think something happened to the world." She gave a brief shiver of apprehension. "Seems like nothing's left but us three and the fog." Then she noticed a clear spot in the road ahead and, relieved, headed toward it.

When she reached the bridge that spanned the gut, Amy stopped to rest, leaning against the wooden railing. The sun had burned the fog into a thin sparkling mist, except in the ravine where it nestled as thick as ever, twining against tree trunks like giant cobwebs, thinning to smoky swirls in the upper branches.

"Our little island ends and the world begins," she said to her daughter, who snuggled against her shoulder, making cooing noises. Amy smiled at the baby, then looked down at the water, deep enough for fish but too shallow for swimming.

"This old gut's a funny creek, Hannah. Flows out of the river down there in the fog and circles right back in again behind our barn. Like its sole purpose in the world is to slice off an island. Over there's where your dad and I made love." She nodded toward a bend in the creek beyond which she and Troy had spread their blanket for a picnic. "No highway marker here to commemorate the occasion, but I bet someday you'll agree it was a mighty significant event." She gave the baby a gentle hug and rocked her back and forth. "Troy's going to love you. No way he'll be able to help himself."

Gazing at the languid stream, Amy noticed a school of minnows near the base of the bridge, then spotted a sweetening bug darting about like a tiny boat without a rudder. "Good thing there's no bass around. You'd be somebody's breakfast by now." Finally she cradled the baby against her neck and continued across the bridge, careful not to trip over any loose planks.

When she reached the other side, the howling made her stop. Glancing around, she saw the hound sitting in the middle of the bridge, head cocked to one side. Bending her knees, she leaned down to pick up a rock, then sighed and stood up again.

"You aren't worth the effort, Elvis. Come on. The sooner we let Troy know we're alone tonight, the sooner he can make plans to come out and see us."

Wearing freshly laundered jeans and her best blouse, Amy sat on the top step of the front porch listening to her portable radio and watching the evening slowly fade into twilight. Her right hand mechanically pushed up and down on the handle of a dilapidated buggy, gently rocking it. Her baby made soft contented noises.

"Must've had to work late," Amy said with little conviction when all the color had drained from the sky.

For a long time she watched the darkening road that lay like a strip of dull yellow tape a shade lighter than the fields it pieced together. When it was almost dark, a cicada began to shrill from the willow in the side yard, and a vague heel print of moon appeared over the river trees, coming and going with the floating, drifting clouds. Amy continued to sit, as though in a trance, her hand still on the buggy. Heat lightning flickered in the west, bringing no thunder.

Suddenly she shoved the buggy against the screen door, then slammed her fists on the porch floor. In an instant she was running through the yard toward the willow. She tripped over a root and fell, then scrambled up and ducked under the foliage. She began unbuttoning her blouse with stiff, jerky movements. The last button refused and she ripped it open. Clutching her right breast with both hands, she squeezed until milk dribbled out, welcoming the pain, hoping it would dull the memory ...

It was past midnight, just three days after she and Troy had made love, and she was lying in bed. She'd been sleeping— she knew that much—but whether she was still asleep and having a dream she wasn't sure.

Her body felt alive with desire, the way it did when she was with Troy. Either she was dreaming he was stroking her in places only he would be allowed to touch or he was actually there, having slipped in through the open window. She felt her nipples being kissed and a hand moving gently between her thighs. Unable to resist any longer, she reached out and drew him close.

When she realized it wasn't Troy, Amy screamed and tried to pull away, but the man had already entered her. He covered her mouth with his mouth and pinned her body to the mattress with his body, thrusting up and down until finally he was spent. Then he sat on the edge of the bed and apologized for what he had done.

"You've gotten so pretty and sexy-looking I couldn't help myself," he said. "I wanted to feel those curves and sweet places just once before you grew up and left the nest. I never intended to do more ... I swear as God is my witness. I wouldn't have if you hadn't encouraged me."

"I was half asleep," Amy sobbed. "I thought you were ..."

"Shhh, it's all right, honey. You didn't do anything wrong and neither did I. These things happen. Just make sure you keep it to yourself. We wouldn't want you mom finding out. It would hurt her feelings something awful ..."

Amy screamed and wrung herself again. When the milk would no longer flow, she wrenched her other breast, shaking her head wildly and sobbing. Finally her legs buckled and she sank to the ground.

Crying quietly, she gazed through the willow's

branches at the nearly starless sky until the hound started licking her face. Without lowering her head, she pushed him away. When he nuzzled up again, she grabbed his ears and squeezed until he finally broke free and scampered back to the house.

Soon the baby began to fuss, the sound drifting into the yard, adding a dissonant voice to the chorus of insects, peepers, and other night creatures that hummed and grated and rattled against the dark.

"Shut up!" Amy yelled.

The crying on the porch grew louder and more demanding, drowning out the night sounds.

OLD WOMEN (1968)

As Cora Hibbard left her house near Ralph Bunche High School, she sensed there was something unusual about the day, something special that set it apart. Whatever was different about this particular Saturday, however, except for traffic being heavier than normal, eluded her.

Cautiously she edged her way down the incline of her yard, one hand lifting the hem of her dress to keep it from catching in her straggly rose bushes, the other clutching a straw hat fringed with wax cherries. Once she reached the street, she put on the hat, adjusted it to shield her eyes from the sun, and began picking her way toward the business district. She had walked only a short distance before a car full of black people approached from behind. Cora waved as it passed and offered a tentative smile, thinking she might know one or two of its occupants. She didn't recognize a soul, however, and nobody waved back. Her smile faded, painful acknowledgment of the fact that whereas she once had known almost every black person in Chockoyotte, now she barely knew a handful.

In the next block she noticed several vehicles parked in front of the Dillard house, and suddenly she thought she knew what was unusual about the day: Clivie Dillard's funeral. A member of the Black Panthers, Clivie had been killed in a shootout with Chicago police and his body sent home to his parents for burial. Still Cora wasn't sure; maybe that was what set today apart, maybe not.

At the railroad tracks she stopped to rest, leaning against the blinker signal that flashed and clanged to warn of approaching trains. Withdrawing a cardboard fan from her pocket, she spread it open and began fanning herself, thinking of her son Lucius, who had left Chockoyotte some thirty years earlier as a porter for the Atlantic Coast Line Railroad. These were the Seaboard tracks she stood beside now, a branch line from Portsmouth to Norlina. The Atlantic Coast Line was a block away and ran above the town on a combination of mounded dirt and steel and wooden trestles, but in Cora's mind the two railroads were one and the rails she stood beside now were the ones that had taken Lucius away. She followed them with her gaze until they disappeared in a roiling of heat waves on the horizon.

Her back propped against the headboard by two pillows, Virginia Gregory was thinking of a time over sixty years ago when her Uncle Jack, a trainer of thoroughbred horses, visited her family. It was as though she were sixteen again and sitting at the dinner table with her father and mother and three brothers listening to this delightful man hold forth on horse racing. She pictured him merely as tall and handsome, the intervening years having blurred any specific recollections about his appearance, although concerning the fact that he looked every bit a gentleman there wasn't the slightest doubt. On the bed beside her, next to her wooden cane, lay the reason for remembering him so poignantly, the slender leather-bound volume *Poems of Emily Dickinson: Third Series* copyrighted by Roberts Brothers in 1896 and edited by Mabel Loomis Todd in 1917. Her uncle had sent it to her shortly after his visit.

She picked up the book and once again read the familiar inscription on the flyleaf: "For my dear niece Virgie. This isn't a book to be read through, but rather one to be dipped into at random for a few minutes refreshment. If you don't find it to your liking, or even if you do, feel free to pass it on to a kindred spirit." Memory surged again and this time she was sitting under a pecan tree outside her girlhood home listening to her uncle expound on the Kentucky Derby one of his horses had almost won ...

"Miz Gregory?"

She placed the book on the bedside table. "Yes. Come in, Sadie."

The door opened and a tall black woman entered the room.

"I'm goin', Miz Gregory. It's almost nine-thirty. I'll be late for the funeral if I don't leave now."

The white woman's brow furrowed. "Hasn't Cora come?"

"Nome. Nary a sign of her. I can't be waitin' around no longer. She was spose to be here a hour ago."

Pulling herself to a sitting position, Virginia reached for the partially-written check on the bedside table, filled in the amount, and held it out. "Thank you for coming, Sadie. I'm sorry for any inconvenience."

The black woman took the check in the same motion that she turned toward the door. "Cora ought not be late like this," she added over her shoulder.

When Virginia heard the back door slam, she hauled herself out of bed and with the help of her cane made her way through the dining room past the mahogany table and matching sideboard, reaching the sunroom just in time to gaze through a window and see Sadie disappear down the driveway. Cora was nowhere in sight.

At Second Street Cora turned directly into the sun, keeping her head low so her hat would shade her eyes. Near the end of the block she stepped from the sidewalk down to the dirt alley that separated the Western Auto from the Silver Screen next door, tilting her head back just long enough to read *In the Heat of the Night*, a film she had never heard of, on the marquee.

"On your way to play Aunt Tom this mornin'?" a voice called.

Cora stopped and gazed into the alley, her hand shielding her eyes from the sun's glare. "Who's that?"

"Little Black Sambo," a different voice replied with

a snicker.

Finally she saw them in the shadows, two young blacks leaning against the brick side of the Western Auto. The taller was dressed in jeans and a faded denim shirt, and the other, who held a bottle in his hand, wore army fatigues and a white tee shirt.

"How come you ain't goin' to the funeral?" the taller boy asked, his words slurred. Without waiting for an answer, he added, "We ain't goin' neither ... but not for the same reason as you."

Cora started to walk on.

"You wait'll I finish!" the voice snapped, catching her in midstep, stopping her. "I ain't splained why we boycottin' Clivie's funeral." The boy shifted weight from one leg to the other before slouching back against the building. "He's bein' laid to rest, that's why. Laid to rest, you unnerstand. Niggers gonna put him in the ground and do a lot of wailin' and hymn singin', and then they'll throw dirt over him and that'll be the end of it." He paused, mouth contorting, lips clenching. "Ah, the lily-livered darkies. You know what we oughta be doin'? We oughta burn down this town. But what do we do? We lay Clivie to rest ... his body and his spirit. In another week everybody'll forgot he ever lived ..."

"You're drunk," Cora said. "You're both drunk and you shouldn't be on the street."

The boy glared at her, his hands clenched and his body rigid, as if he were about to attack her. But then, as though a great weariness suddenly came over him, he heaved a sigh and grabbed the bottle from his companion. "You right about that, granma," he said and tilted the bottle to his mouth.

"Still goin' in at the back door?" the other boy asked, looking at Cora with an air of aloof disdain.

At first she didn't understand. Her hand still raised against the sun, she stood in silence, staring past the movie theater, the direction she wanted to go.

"You still goin' in ole lady Gregory's back door?" the boy repeated, casually sarcastic. "I used to see you when I mowed grass for some of them rich crackers 'round there."

Finally she realized what he meant. "I don't need to go in the front door to prove something I knew before you were born," she declared.

The young black hooked his thumbs into the pockets of his army fatigues, his smile expanding into a mocking grin. "And what might that be?"

Cora hesitated. "That I'm a lady," she said through trembling lips. "A colored lady."

Both boys guffawed. The taller one looked at her with a mixture of urgency and impatience. "What if all black people acted like you the last twenty years, bowin' and scrapin' and sayin' yessuh and nosuh to the almighty white folks? We'd still be pickin' cotton for ole Massah. Pickaninnies. You know that?"

"If I need your guidance on what to realize, young man," Cora said, her voice quavering, "I'll ask for it." She moved across the alley and up onto the sidewalk, pretending his words had no effect on her.

"Times are changin', ole woman," the voice knifed after her. "But you ain't changin' with 'em. You been left way behind. You a whole lot worse than those darkies at Clivie Dillard's funeral. You ain't no lady. You ain't nothin' atall but a white woman's nigger—a burden to your own people."

Turning from the window, Virginia Gregory left the sunroom and slowly made her way to the library with its shelves of Harvard Classics on one side and law books on the other. On the wall above the fireplace was a portrait of her husband, the white-haired man looking handsome and dignified. She'd had it painted from a small photograph after he died, overseeing the job herself until the artist had everything the way she wanted. She went over to the portrait.

"Such a strong-willed man," she said. "Who would believe I once had the nerve to humble you?"

It was the first year of their marriage, but she visualized the scene as if it were happening now. During a discussion concerning the naming of their first child—she wanted Jack in honor of her uncle if it was a boy, while her husband felt the name too commonplace—the man had cursed her. "Damn you, Virginia! Damn you and your stubbornness!"

She was so shocked at his language that without realizing the audacity of what she was saying she ordered him not only to apologize but to do it on his knees. Then suddenly she realized she had demanded something he would never do. The shock of his profanity all but forgotten in the horror of her own reaction, she sought some way to save face before her husband annihilated her with laughter. But to her amazement he never showed the slightest inclination toward ridiculing her preposterous demand. After the initial look of surprise, a boyish apologetic expression crept over his face and he knelt in front of her as though at an altar and asked her forgiveness ...

The sound of the telephone startled her back to the present. It rang three times before she was able to put herself in motion and three more before she managed to retrace her steps to the sunroom and pick up the receiver.

It was her daughter-in-law Mary calling to say she and Jack wouldn't be able to visit tomorrow after all. There was just too much happening right now. Jack was working on an important case that was going to trial earlier than expected, and she had lots of last minute shopping to do for Jack Junior. "I hope you haven't gone to a lot of trouble getting ready for us. We'll come see you soon. Next weekend is out, though. That's when we're taking Jack Junior to Chapel Hill. Can you believe freshman orientation is just a week away? The summer has really flown by, hasn't it? Anyway, we'll call and let you know for sure when we can come ..."

After hanging up the receiver, Virginia slowly returned to the library, stopping at the coffee table where she kept her scrapbook. Neatly folded between the worn cover and the first page was the newspaper clipping showing her husband on the day he set out his shingle to practice law in Chockoyotte. She had presented the clipping, along with a generous check, as a high school graduation gift to Jack Junior the last time she saw him. Her grandson forgot the clipping when he left, but he did remember to take the check.

Prominently featured on the scrapbook's first page was Virginia's wedding picture, and she gazed at the two young people in wonderment. So many years had passed since then, it seemed as if she had stepped into a time machine and, before she knew what was happening, a half century had sped by and Charles was gone ...

She felt like crying. Knowing Cora might arrive any moment, she fought back the tears, not wanting to be seen in such a pitiful state. Wasn't there something she needed to do—a bill to pay, a room to tidy, a magazine subscription to renew? Not really. The work in preparation for Jack and Mary's visit had already been done, as had all her other weekly chores. There *was* something she could do now, though, a small task but an important one. She had originally planned it for the afternoon, but there was no point in waiting until then, every reason to do it now. Gently closing the scrapbook, she shuffled off toward her bedroom to look for scissors and paper.

It took Cora another ten minutes to walk from the Silver Screen to the familiar house on Sycamore Street. She moved as though in a daze, the words "white woman's nigger" and "burden to your own people" ringing in her head. Perspiration dripped from her face, but too many troubling thoughts were running through her mind to think of her fan.

The boy was wrong about her relationship with Mrs. Gregory, she kept telling herself. She recalled their many pleasant evenings together reminiscing about times past or reading aloud from books by authors such as Rudyard Kipling, Walt Whitman, Mark Twain, and Robert Frost, volumes Cora had come to prize almost as much as Mrs. Gregory did. For a moment as she gazed at the rear of the sprawling two-story house, she was almost convinced that, like the books, it partly belonged to her, that her presence there was much more than that of a servant to a white woman not even as old as she. But the original question of the boy in the alley came hauntingly back to her, and she wondered if he might be right after all.

Suddenly the house blurred and Cora felt faint. Knowing she had to get out of the sun, she moved with effort across the yard and slowly mounted the stoop, her right hand clutching the iron railing. On the last step she paused, realizing for the first time that Sadie Capps, the woman who spent Friday nights with Mrs. Gregory to allow Cora one night a week in her own home, would have wanted to attend Clivie Dillard's funeral. With a sigh she opened the screen door and pulled herself onto the back porch, preparing for Sadie's wrath.

The door to the kitchen was open. Expecting Sadie to appear any moment, Cora slowly entered the room and was surprised to find Mrs. Gregory sitting at the small wooden table between the refrigerator and the stove.

"Good morning," the white woman said and began pulling herself up with the aid of her cane.

"Mrs. Gregory," Cora acknowledged, exhausted, stopping just past the door and leaning against the stove. "Where's ... ? Oh, she's gone." A momentary sense of relief washed over her. "Is that it? She couldn't wait for me any longer?"

The white woman didn't answer. As she moved toward the pantry, she lost her balance, teetered, then regained her equilibrium.

"Careful," Cora warned. "Want me to help you?"

"No, thank you. I can manage."

As Virginia disappeared through the pantry doorway, Cora poured herself a glass of water and drank it. Then she went to the table and eased herself into the vacated chair. Thinking Mrs. Gregory was angry at her for being late, she started to call out and say she couldn't bear any more ill feelings, but then she heard the shuffle of footsteps.

"I have something for you."

Cora gazed at the small gift-wrapped package, wondering why she was being handed what looked like a present. Suddenly it dawned on her what made the day special.

"Happy birthday, Cora."

Taking the gift, she read the card which simply repeated what Mrs. Gregory had just said.

"Aren't you going to open it?"

As though the words were a command, Cora began tearing at the paper. Realizing there was something she wanted to know before she opened the package, she looked up at the woman standing beside her.

"Mrs. Gregory?"

"Yes."

"Nevermind."

When Cora realized what the book was, she stared at it in disbelief. "You can't give me this. It's ... it's too precious to you. Weren't you planning to leave it to your grandson?"

"I want you to have it. I've written your name in it and an inscription."

Cora turned to the flyleaf in the front of the book

and read beneath the original inscription the words: "For my friend Cora Hibbard on her 78th birthday."

Cora's first impulse was to stand up and give the woman a hug. Before she did or said anything more, though, there really was something she wanted to know.

"Mrs. Gregory, what would you have done if ..."

"Yes. Go on."

"If ..." But the possibility of further pain was too great a risk. The birthday would have to be enough, Cora told herself, taking consolation in the fact that the other had not only remembered but given her such a wonderful present. "It's not important," she said and gazed at the book. "Thank you, Mrs. Gregory."

"You're most welcome."

Detecting a note of sadness in Cora's manner, Virginia wondered if she would have been happier with a more conventional gift, something new like the attractive snow globe advertised in the latest Montgomery Ward catalog. At least a present like that could never be considered a hand-me-down. No, that's not it, Virginia decided as she sat down across the table from Cora. She's probably just overtired—and no wonder after having made such a long walk.

Virginia thought of a recent article in the local paper about the mom and pop taxi company that just opened in Chockoyotte, and she made a mental note to suggest Cora make use of its services. Right now, though, there was something else she wanted to talk to Cora about, an issue that had concerned Virginia for quite some time. *Since you are probably the best friend I have, doesn't it make sense to start calling me by my first name?* she planned to ask. *And wouldn't it be appropriate that a friend of mine should be able to enter and exit this home through the front door as well as the back?*

Virginia had been reluctant to bring up such an awkward subject. Implementing this radical change would surely be difficult for Cora, at least at first, and it was always possible the change would end up eroding an already "satisfactory" relationship. If it ain't broke, as her dead husband used to delight in saying, don't attempt to fix it. In addition, there were the neighbors to think about. How would they react to such a change? And more importantly, what would Jack and Mary think about it? Still it was the right thing to do, and Virginia had made up her mind to broach the subject on Cora's birthday. The book of poems and the inscription she would write on the flyleaf should provide the perfect segue for their ensuing conversation.

Now, however, Virginia was having serious second thoughts. Something was bothering Cora. If anything, she seemed more troubled now than she had been before receiving the birthday gift, definitely in no mood to entertain a radical new idea. Even the idea itself had started losing some of its luster for Virginia. Did it really make sense to change a relationship most people probably would consider ideal?

"You don't seem like yourself today, Cora," she said in a gentle voice. "I don't mean to pry, but is there something wrong?"

Cora looked up from the pages she had been absently turning. You can still ask her, she told herself. Speak now or forever hold your peace.

"I ... I think the heat got the better of me," she finally said. "I'm not as young as I used to be," she added with a weak smile.

"That's a mighty long walk from your home to this one, especially for someone our age. Have you ever thought about taking a cab? There's a taxi service right here in town now. Totem Taxi, I believe it's called."

Cora nodded. "Taking a cab can be expensive, Mrs. Gregory."

"I doubt one to and from your house would cost all that much, especially since the cab won't have to come from Roanoke Falls. At least think about it, Cora. Regardless of what the fare costs, I'll be glad to pay it."

"That's mighty generous of you, Mrs. Gregory," Cora replied after a moment, touched by the other's offer in spite of her own melancholy feelings. "I will give it some thought. Yes, ma'am, I surely will."

Although Cora seemed almost back to her old self now, it was Virginia's turn to feel downhearted, having reached the conclusion that it would probably be better, after all, if she simply let well enough alone.

TIME TO HANG IT UP (1970)

The first thing Ed Mulligan felt upon regaining consciousness was severe discomfort, as though he'd woken up with a bad case of the flu. The area directly behind his eyes throbbed, as did his forehead. His neck, shoulders, and back ached, especially his back. His throat felt like it had been scraped with sandpaper.

Opening his eyes, Ed saw a shimmering blur in the near darkness above him. The rapidly turning blades of a ceiling fan? He couldn't be sure. All he knew for certain was he felt like hell and was lying face up on a hard surface. Must be a bed, he thought, although it was much harder than the one he slept on. He noticed a whirring sound, its pitch increasing as he inhaled, decreasing as he exhaled. Something scraped against his face, tubing of some sort attached to his nostrils. He tried to pull it off but couldn't move his arms. He began to panic.

The area Ed occupied was windowless and tiny,

smaller than the bedroom in his trailer. Curtains hung down on both sides of where he lay. He heard a scraping noise followed by faint rustling as though someone had pushed back a chair in the process of standing up. Out of the corner of his eye, Ed detected a shape, someone moving toward him, a woman. When he tried to sit up, his body didn't respond.

Finally realizing where he was and why he was there, Ed screamed. The hoarse sound coming from his parched throat wasn't even loud enough to compete with the hum of the oxygen machine in the corner.

Eighteen hours earlier Ed had also awakened to discomfort. His head throbbed, not unusual for a Saturday morning except other parts of his body ached as well, especially his right knee. Must have really tied one on last night, he mused, though exactly where he had done the tying escaped him. He did recall some dickhead suggesting he get a job at Jamison Valve because the company had a mixed league where males batted opposite handed and each team had to play at least three females. "You could start for a team like that," the guy chuckled. Ed had taken a drunken swing at him, missed, and toppled heavily over a bar stool, banging his knee against a leg of the pool table.

Slowly he eased himself out of bed, discovering in the process that, except for one sock, he was naked. He tried to remove the sock but was too stove up to reach his foot. How can I show Joe I've still got what it takes when I'm feeling like this? he wondered. Glancing at the clock on the chest of drawers, he saw that practice was only an hour away. Christ, he thought. Practice for guys in the starting lineup was one thing, but for a fifty-two-year-old utility player with a hangover it was quite another.

Deciding to postpone his decision about practice until after breakfast, Ed hobbled into the hallway. Through a window he noticed his truck next to the trailer's patio. He never parked it there. Who the hell had driven him home?

"Who the hell cares?" he muttered and limped on down the hall to the bathroom. "What the fuck difference does it make?"

Bending over with a groan, he turned on the shower, adjusting the water to what he thought would be a comfortable temperature. But when he climbed into the tub, the spray was freezing. He let out a yell and played with the knobs. The water quickly turned hot, causing Ed to jerk backwards, slip, and almost fall, wrenching his already sore knee in the process. "Goddamnit! Doesn't anything in this fuckin' world ever work right?"

As though in answer, the water warmed to a comfortable temperature.

Heaving an angry sigh, Ed thought of his performance two nights earlier when he played second base in place of Jake Futch, who had taken the wife and kids to Virginia Beach. Since their coach didn't like guys missing games, Ed might have earned back a starting spot if he'd played well, but he had gone two for four—not particularly good for slow-pitch softball—and had let two grounders skip past him into right field. His second error had cost his team the game.

After showering, Ed fixed coffee and toast but hardly touched the toast. For a while he limped up and down the trailer, a cigarette in one hand and his coffee mug in the other, trying to work the soreness out of his knee and the stiffness out of the rest of his body. "Maybe it's time to hang it up," he muttered as he paced down the hallway.

He went outside to get the paper. His breath plumes of white smoke, he stood shirtless on the patio and gazed down the row of trailers at a grove of trees in the distance, the maples already starting to turn. He noticed a postal truck pull up to the row of mailboxes, thinking that the only thing he would get today besides junk mail would be another reminder to vacate the premises by the end of the month. Letting the cold seep into his skin, he watched the truck as it pulled away from the mailboxes and disappeared down the dirt road. The thought that this was a great way to catch pneumonia almost made him laugh.

Back inside his trailer, Ed thumbed through the sports section, finding nothing of interest, not even the article about the upcoming World Series between Sparky Anderson's Big Red Machine and Earl Weaver's Baltimore Orioles. Why read it when every player mentioned would have achieved on the highest level what he no longer could accomplish on the lowest: be in the starting lineup of a ball team?

Ed had always been a starter, going all the way back to Little League when he was chosen as an all-star the last two years he played. Then came two stellar seasons in Pony League and three at Chockoyotte High School where his senior year he batted almost .400

and was voted All-Conference honorable mention. After that, he had played over three decades of quality softball in the Roanoke Falls Industrial League, starting every single game until this year.

"I figure I'll use you as my number one utility man," Joe Mangum, his coach, told him at the beginning of the season. "Anybody doesn't show up for a game, you'll play his position, unless it's shortstop or centerfield. If one of those guys is out, I'll shift somebody else to that spot and you can play what's open."

"You're benching me, Joe … after all these years?" Ed had said, then tried to make light of the situation. "Say it ain't so, Joe."

"I took myself out of the lineup three years ago, Ed. You're two years older than me. We're not spring chickens anymore. We don't have the reflexes of these young bucks."

Joe was right, of course. Although still a decent hitter, Ed was a liability on defense. And it wasn't a matter of working hard over the winter to get in shape for the following season. Next spring he wouldn't be as good as he is now.

He decided to skip practice, figuring it was too much to ask of his aching carcass. Why put himself through more grief when the season was almost over and he probably wouldn't start another game regardless of how well he did in practice. He limped back into the kitchen and picked up the phone.

"Hell," he said and slammed down the receiver. "Let him find out the way he does from most of his young bucks—when they don't show up."

Lighting another cigarette, Ed paced some more around the trailer, ending up back in the kitchen where he considered washing the three days of dishes piled in the sink.

"Ah, let 'em rot," he said, then picked up the phone again and started to call Harriet Beasley, planning to invite her over for a few games of gin rummy. Pausing in mid dial, Ed weighed the consequences. She would probably try to get him in the sack, and he wasn't interested in that, any more than he'd been last night. He remembered now—he had been at the Shamrock with Harriet and she had driven him home. After undressing him and putting him to bed, she had removed her clothes and climbed in after him, only to climb back out a moment later when he told her he thought he was going to puke.

He hung up the phone. The last thing he needed now was to be smothered by a fifty-four-year-old nymphomaniac with halitosis and sagging, leathery tits.

Two cups of coffee and several cigarettes later, Ed found himself staring at the nearly-empty coffee pot. He had given it to Dorothy, his first wife, as a birthday present the year before he ran off to Nevada with Ramona Higgins. The memory deepened his gloom. He went back to the bedroom where he opened the top drawer of his dresser and took out a stack of pictures. Some were of Dorothy and some were of their daughter Samantha. He looked at them until they blurred through his tears. Then he put them gently back in the drawer and got out the letter to Dorothy he had written a few weeks earlier, after finding out his trailer was going to be repossessed.

Slowly and carefully he reread it, discovering that his apology didn't sound nearly as poignant as when he'd written it, though it did say pretty much what he wanted Dorothy to know. The last paragraph sent a chill up his spine, but he took comfort in the fact that he could always leave that part out when he typed the letter. He would definitely type it. Dorothy would appreciate the extra effort.

When he reached the old Seaboard tracks—now a part of the Seaboard-Coast Line system—Ed had to stop for a slow-moving freight. He put his truck in neutral and tried to do the same with his mind, leaning his head against the worn headrest and gazing at the passing freight cars. Next to him on the seat was a half-empty pint of Jim Beam. He thought about taking a swig but decided to wait. As a string of empty flat cars rumbled by, Ed glimpsed the top of the trestle bridge he would soon cross on his way to Roanoke Falls. He thought of a similar bridge some thirty miles downriver, the one on a lonely stretch of road near Scotland Neck where Samantha had died on an icy January night when her boyfriend's car skidded into the concrete abutment. The car was so old it didn't even have seat belts.

The sound of beeping nudged him back to the present. Realizing the train had passed and the driver behind him was tooting his horn, Ed slowly put the truck in gear and eased across the tracks.

On the outskirts of Roanoke Falls, he passed Jamison Valve, the company he had worked for back when it was located next to the Coca Cola plant in Chockoyotte and employed barely a handful of people. He tried to ignore the place, but just being in the vicinity of the modern glass and steel structure and immaculately kept grounds filled him with disgust.

Two blocks later he turned left and the area quickly deteriorated. He passed a low-rent apartment complex, a dingy-looking fuel oil dealership, and the baseball field where he had played Pony League, long since grown up with weeds. After crossing a spur track, its rails blacktopped over, he pulled into a rutted driveway and parked next to a cinderblock building not much larger than a garage. "Mulligan Screw Products" said the faded sign above the padlocked door. "Property of Wachovia Bank and Trust Company" proclaimed a newer sign stapled to the door. "Auction to be held October 10th."

Taking the liquor bottle with him, Ed went around to the back of the building and slipped in through a window with a broken pane. Once inside he rummaged around in a closet until he located the second-hand typewriter he had bought for the secretary he could never afford to hire. After finding some paper in the room's only desk, he started to drink some bourbon but again decided to wait, realizing he would probably need all his faculties to type the letter. Sitting down at the desk, he rolled a sheet of paper onto the carriage, then withdrew Dorothy's letter from his shirt pocket.

"Fuck it," he said and unscrewed the cap and tilted the bottle to his mouth.

The bourbon soon began to relax him, and he found himself reflecting on things not altogether unpleasant, starting with his high school typing teacher and her long jet-black hair and shapely body. He had signed up for her class because she was young and sexy and he thought her course would be a snap. It wasn't. She taught like a drill sergeant, and by the end of the semester Ed was sweating out forty words a minute. He saw her now peering at the wall clock, waiting for the second hand to reach the twelve so she could tell the class to BEGIN.

He took another swig of bourbon. The memory of the teacher faded, replaced by Ramona Higgins, his second wife. Ed was lying in bed at the Las Vegas motel where they had gone for their honeymoon, and Ramona was walking toward him wearing nothing but red lace panties. As she bent down to kiss him, she paused momentarily to let her blond hair dance seductively in his face, and he cupped his hands around the most voluptuous breasts he had ever seen. Their marriage lasted six months, just long enough for Ed to realize Ramona was shacking up with Ted Jamison, the owner of Jamison Valve.

He put her out of his mind. Other women drifted into his consciousness, mostly ones he'd gone out with after his second divorce. There were one or two good lookers, but most were like Harriet Beasley, has-beens or never-weres. Now that Ed was in no immediate danger from Harriet's breath, he thought of her with a degree of affection, realizing that of all the women he'd ever known, she would probably be the only one to give a rip whether he lived or died.

That wasn't exactly true, he told himself. Dorothy would still care. That thought, however, brought little consolation. As soon as he realized he and Ramona were history, he had telephoned Dorothy, only to learn that she was engaged to a guy from Enfield, a wimpy-looking insurance salesman, it turned out, who probably wouldn't dare set foot in a place like the Shamrock. She should have known he'd come crawling back.

Ed recalled the last time he talked to Dorothy. It was at Samantha's funeral. Dorothy had arranged everything, so all he had to do was show up.

"You look real pretty," he told her after the service. She had aged more than gracefully, looking almost beautiful in her dark blue suit and matching shoes. "Marriage—I mean your second one—seems to agree with you."

She thanked him for the compliment and asked if he was making a go of his machine shop.

"Business has picked up," he lied. "I got two guys working for me now." He neglected to tell her that one of the guys was a part-time employee and the other a retired engineer he met at Alcoholics Anonymous who came in once a week to help with quotes. When she asked if he still played softball, Ed told her he did. "I had the highest batting average on the team last year," he proudly said.

He had intended to apologize for leaving her and tell her it was the worst mistake of his life, but somehow it just didn't seem right bringing up the subject at their daughter's funeral.

After mailing the letter at the post office, Ed slowly walked back to his truck. He had included the last paragraph exactly as written, but before typing it he went in the shop area and gazed at the pathetic machinery, none of it automated, the ancient lathe, screw machine, and chucker all purchased second or third hand from companies in the process of upgrading their equipment. The thought that he would never again operate one of those antiquated machines or teach some other poor slob how to do it wasn't exactly unappealing.

"Give me one good reason not to do it!" he shouted across the concrete floor, holding the liquor bottle aloft for emphasis. He almost smiled as the echo came reverberating back: "Do it ... do it ..."

While parked next to the post office, Ed polished off the last of the bourbon, then started the truck's engine and slowly drove through Roanoke Falls, giving the alcohol a chance to work. By the time he reached Jamison Valve, he had on a good buzz. Too proud to look, he raised the middle finger of his right hand in a final casual salute.

Outside the city limits he picked up speed, his old truck starting to rattle and shimmy as it neared forty miles an hour. When the Roanoke River swung into view, he pressed down the accelerator. The truck sputtered, then surged ahead, the motor straining, the floorboards shaking. About a hundred yards from the bridge, he glanced at the speedometer and saw he was going almost fifty-five. That should be fast enough, he decided, assuming he hit square.

His eyes focused on the right concrete abutment, locking in on it as though he were a kamikaze pilot and the bridge his target. About fifty yards away he wondered if he might be making a mistake. His right foot lifted and he thought of Harriet Beasley. Not all their time together had been unpleasant. Maybe with a different hairdo and a little dental work ...

"Piss on it," he said and floored the accelerator. "She's as washed up as I am."

"Take it easy, Ed. It's just me. I've been sitting with you most of the night. You had a bad accident and you're in the intensive care unit at the county hospital. But there's some good news. The doctor said you're definitely going to live."

Ed let out a long, slow moan of despair and tried to turn his head away, only managing to rotate it an inch or two on the pillow. "Good news, hell. I was trying to kill myself."

Harriet looked astonished. "But ... but you had your seat belt on. The doctor said if you hadn't been wearing one, you'd have been a goner for sure."

"I did what! Oh, Jesus ... I couldn't even get that right."

For a while the only sound came from the oxygen machine. "I don't think you really wanted to kill yourself," Harriet offered in a low, tentative voice.

"The hell I didn't. I must've buckled up out of habit."

"Well, maybe you did. But whatever the reason, you're still alive. And I for one am grateful." She moved closer and took hold of Ed's hand. "I know you've got financial problems, but you can deal with that. I'll help you."

"It's not just the shop. I lost the trailer too. I've lost everything."

There was a long pause. "Well, for whatever it might be worth ... if anything ... you've still got me."

Ed tried to roll his eyes but they hurt so much all he could do was squint. "I ... I can't move anything but my head. Did the doctor say anything about me being ... paralyzed?"

"He said there's almost a hundred percent chance you'll regain the use of your upper body."

"My upper body? What about the rest of me?"

Harriet took a deep breath and slowly let it out in an almost inaudible sigh.

"Tell me, damn it. I've got a right to know."

"The doctor said ... he said it's too early to tell about that. He said it's possible you'll be able to make a complete recovery, but ..."

"But what?"

"You've got to have a spine operation, maybe two of them, and a lot of things have to go right."

"So I'll probably be stuck in a damn wheelchair the rest of my life."

"You don't know that. Good things do happen, Ed. They happen all the time."

"Yeah, right. So do disasters. It's all a matter of luck, Harriet. The little bit I had ran out when I strapped on that goddamn seat belt."

The silence that followed lasted nearly a minute. During that time Ed bit down on his lower lip and stared at the ceiling, his bloodshot eyes showing almost as much anger as fear. Harriet's eyes filled with tears, and she wiped them away with the back of her hand.

"I know you're in a really bad place right now," she said. "Whether you get better or not, you're going to need someone to take care of you, at least for a while. I'd like to be that person, Ed. You can stay at my place for as long as you like. No strings attached." She leaned over and kissed him on the forehead and once again gently took hold of his hand. "I know I'm not exactly a prize. But I'm not a dog either." She hesitated. "Am I?"

Ed didn't answer her right away. "No," he finally said and managed to squeeze her hand ever so slightly. "You're not."

JUST PASSING THROUGH (1973)

Randy Matthews, his shoulder-length blond hair parted in the middle, was looking for a place to eat. Noticing a sign on a store-front window that said "Wilson's Café," he pulled into a parking space in front of the adjacent barber shop, got out of his aging Volkswagen van plastered with peace symbols, and headed for the door.

Since he thought he was still in the white section of Chockoyotte, Randy was shocked to find only black people in the restaurant. There were seven of them, including the young waitress behind the counter who was chatting with a boy about Randy's age. Also sitting at the counter was an old man in bib overalls, his short wiry hair looking as though it had been sprinkled with talcum powder. A heavy set man who looked to be in his mid-to-late thirties sat at a nearby table reading a newspaper, and an elderly couple occupied a booth not far from a silent jukebox.

Randy's first impulse was to return to his van and look for another restaurant. To do so, however, would suggest he was a typical bigot who was either afraid of black people or felt above eating with them, and he didn't want to leave either impression. Since none of the restaurant's occupants seemed hostile, he closed the door and made his way to a corner booth, sliding into the seat next to a pinball machine.

As yet none of the blacks had given any indication they were aware of Randy's presence. It was as if they hadn't noticed him, though he was sure they had; most of them had looked up when he opened the door. But they had gone back to whatever they were doing, showing no interest in him, as though the door had been opened and closed by the wind. For an instant he had an urge to call to the waitress, not to hurry her but to let her and the rest of the black people in the restaurant know he was there. Eventually she ended her conversation with the black boy and came over to Randy's booth.

"Take your order?" she asked, extracting a pad and pencil from her apron.

"Hi," Randy said, disappointed when she didn't return his smile. "Guess I'll have a cheeseburger and …"

"What you want on it?"

"Uh, all the way. And an order of fries."

"To drink?"

He wanted to tell her to slow down and give him a chance to think, maybe let him make small talk like he did with waitresses at the Rathskeller in Chapel Hill where he and his friends sometimes went on the weekend or to unwind after an exam. She hadn't even offered him a menu.

"Oh, a Coke or a Pepsi. Either one's fine."

As the waitress walked back to the counter, the black man with the newspaper asked her for a cup of coffee.

"Sure, Mr. Wilson. Soon as I give Albert this order."

A moment later Randy noticed the black boy get up from the counter and head in his direction, walking with a swagger. Randy nodded politely as he approached, but the boy ignored him and went to the pinball machine. He inserted a quarter and began to play, the ball rolling and ricocheting under the glass as numbers clicked across the scoreboard.

The boy was halfway through his second game when the waitress brought Randy's lunch.

"Thank you," he said. "It looks delicious."

She totaled the cost of the meal, tore the check from her pad, and placed it face up on the table. Without looking at him, she turned and headed back to the counter.

"Rowena, you forget my coffee?" the man with the newspaper asked.

Surprise animated the waitress' face, then remembrance. "Sorry about that, Mr. Wilson. I'll get it for you right now."

As she poured the man's coffee, the waitress apologized again and gave him a warm smile, surprising Randy because it was so different from her impersonal treatment of him. The pinball machine gave a heavy thunk and went silent, and he knew the young black had won a free game.

"Hey, honky. How's that burger taste?"

Slowly Randy turned around. The boy was staring at him, looking mischievous or hostile, Randy couldn't tell which. "Good. Real good."

"I heard Rowena tell Albert to give it his special treatment. That means he seasoned it with spit."

After glancing at what was left of his cheeseburger, Randy set it on the plate. He lifted the glass of cola to his lips.

"Probably peed in that. Generally Albert don't stop with the main dish."

Randy gave the boy a feeble smile. "You sure know how to ruin a person's appetite," he said, setting the glass back on the table.

"What you doin' in here anyway?" the boy asked.

"Eating lunch ... or trying to."

"Why here?"

"Why not here? This is a restaurant and I was hungry."

"You from 'round here?"

"Elizabeth City."

"You eat with niggers down there too?"

The question surprised Randy. He didn't know how to answer, either way foreseeing trouble. "I don't think that term applies to anybody," he finally said. "At least I never use it."

"Is that right? Me, I say it all the time. Must be you don't like niggers. That true, honky?"

"My name's Randy. And, no, it's not true. Absolutely not."

"Then what you really doin' in here, man—

slummin'?"

"That's enough," a voice called, the man who had been reading the paper. "Last thing I need in here is a racial incident. Now cool it, both of you."

The young black muttered something under his breath, then gave Randy a final glare before returning his attention to the pinball machine and readying it for the free game. He fired a ball into play with such velocity it bounced across the top three times before dropping into the scoring area.

A half hour earlier when Randy pulled into a parking space in front of Swenson's Barber Shop, Shag Draper, a laid-off cotton mill worker, happened to be staring out the plate-glass window.

"Well, well, would you look at that. I'm not sure if it's male or female or maybe even a sheepdog, but I think you've got yourself a customer, Glen."

Glen Swenson, a large man with huge hands, was sitting in the first of two barber chairs reading the *Roanoke News*. He glanced out the window and shook his head in disgust. "If I wasn't so hard up for business, I wouldn't let a long-haired punk like that in my shop."

"You might not have to. Looks like he's headed for Levi's place. When he realizes it's full of niggers, he'll be out of there lickety split."

"Damn those people anyway," Swenson said. "Wasn't for them, I wouldn't have to close this place."

"Are you sure there's no way you could keep it open? It don't seem right not having a barber shop in downtown Chockoyotte."

"You saw how many customers I had this morning.

I'm lucky if I get five a day. Most everybody goes to Roanoke Falls ... them that still gets haircuts."

"Well, at least you can still work out of your house. You might do better there than you think."

"I doubt it. Wouldn't surprise me if I have to get out of the barbering business altogether."

"I see you still got that other chair. Thought you had it sold."

"I do. The buyer hasn't picked it up yet. Guess what I got for it, Shag. Take a guess."

"Oh, I don't know. Seems like it'd bring at least a hundred bucks."

"I got twenty."

"That's terrible. Who'd you sell it to?"

"A nigger barber. It was the only offer I got. That's a laugh, ain't it? The niggers force you out, and then they buy up your equipment dirt cheap. Things sure have come to a pretty past."

"It's gonna get worse, too. In another ten years there won't be a white establishment in this entire block. Hell, in twenty years Chockoyotte'll be black as the ace of spades and Levi Wilson will probably be the mayor."

"It's a pity what's happening to this town, Shag ... a damn shame."

"There's a difference between a pity and a damn shame, Glen," Draper said after a brief pause. "I thought you knew that."

"Well, I don't."

Draper's face twisted into a wry grin. "It's a pity if a bus load of niggers and hippies falls off a cliff and everybody on board is killed." He paused momentarily for effect. "It's a damn shame if there was a single empty seat."

As the young black played his free game, Randy resumed eating, having decided the boy must have been joking about the foreign substances in his food, hoping he was anyway. The boy didn't say anything more to him, and when his game was over, he sauntered out of the restaurant. A moment later Randy placed two dollars on the table as a tip, almost as much as the meal cost, picked up his check, and went to the counter. He handed the check and a five-dollar bill to the waitress and waited as she opened the cash register and gave him change.

"Thanks, Rowena," he said. "I really enjoyed the meal."

She nodded vaguely, then turned away.

Standing in front of the cash register, Randy was torn between two desires. Part of him wanted to leave this restaurant and forget about these people, yet he was reluctant to go, feeling a need to establish some kind of meaningful contact with them before exiting their lives forever.

"Uh, Rowena," he said.

The waitress turned around. "Yeah?"

"Can I have a cup of coffee?"

"To go?"

"To drink here if that's OK."

"What you want in it?"

"Black," Randy said, then cringed, sorry he'd used that word. Maybe it would offend coming from him. The young woman might resent his using it as he knew black people deeply resented whites saying the word "nigger," while blacks could apparently say it, as the boy had done, whenever they pleased.

The waitress set a cup of coffee on the counter and moved away. Randy wished she had given him one last chance to make conversation, just small talk anyone might make with another human being. She was already down at the other end of the counter talking to the old man with powdery-looking hair.

Randy focused his attention on the man with the newspaper. After a brief hesitation he walked over to his table.

"Mind if I join you?"

The man regarded him over the top of the paper. "Suit yourself," he said and went back to reading.

Randy sat down and took a sip of coffee. "I take it you're the owner of this restaurant."

The man didn't look up. "Me and the bank. Mostly the bank."

"It's a nice place."

"Thanks." He went on reading the paper.

"How'd ole Hammerin' Hank do last night?" Randy asked after a moment of awkward silence.

"Who?"

"Hank Aaron." Surely this black man would be interested in the Braves slugging right fielder who before the year was over would almost assuredly break Babe Ruth's home run record.

"I have no idea." Without looking up, the man pushed the sports section across the table.

Randy stared at it in disbelief. "What is it with you people?" he asked in frustration. "Why are you so hostile when all I've done is try to be friendly?"

The man put down the section of the paper he had been reading. When Randy saw the smile on his face, he felt as though he'd finally completed a long and arduous initiation. "I'm a junior at Carolina and I'm headed home for the weekend to see my girlfriend," he explained. "I stopped here because I was hungry. If I'd known it was a ... a Negro restaurant, I wouldn't have come in."

"A Tar Heel, huh? Why'd you stick around after you saw everybody in here was black?"

Randy hesitated, both annoyed and intimidated by the question. Still the man didn't seem angry, merely curious. "I didn't want ..." he began, flustered. "I didn't want you folks to think I was a bigot."

The man reached in his shirt pocket, pulled out a pack of cigarettes, and lit one. "In other words, you thought your presence would make our day."

What's the matter with this guy, with all these people? "No," Randy protested. "I ... I just wanted to show you I don't believe in color, that's all. I don't believe in categorizing any group of people. As far as I'm concerned, we're all human beings, whites and blacks, rich and poor."

"If you really believe that, why go somewhere else if you'd known this was a Negro restaurant?" The man exaggerated the pronunciation of the word *Negro*, making it sound like a parody of the way Randy had said it.

This is ridiculous, Randy felt, absolutely ridiculous. Why did he have to justify his actions, especially since he was the one who should receive the apology? Still he felt compelled to explain. "I ... I didn't think I'd be wanted."

The man nodded as though everything should now be perfectly clear. "Seems to me you just answered your own question." He took a drag of his cigarette and set it in the ashtray next to his coffee cup, then picked up the paper and went back to reading.

Randy sat in silence, staring at what he could see of the man's indifferent face. "I'm sorry," he finally said. "I know I don't understand a lot about black people's plight. But I am sympathetic, and I'm making an effort to learn. I'm even taking a course in black literature this semester. I'm going to do a paper on Richard Wright."

As soon as the words were out, Randy knew he had said the wrong thing.

The man put down the newspaper, stubbed out his cigarette, and picked up his coffee cup. "When I was at Shaw University, I wrote a paper on Walt Whitman," he said, getting up from the table. "But I didn't expect white folks to love me for it."

His face flushed with embarrassment, Randy watched the man set his cup on the counter and exit through a doorway in the back of the café. After a while he got up and headed for the front door.

The waitress's voice caught him just as his hand touched the knob. "You haven't paid for your coffee yet."

When he turned around, Randy saw she wasn't even looking at him. "How much?" he asked as he returned to the counter. "A quarter? Or do you charge white people extra?"

When Randy emerged from the restaurant, Glen Swenson and Shag Draper were waiting. They knew the young man must have eaten lunch there, and that, coupled with the length and style of his hair, was all they needed to know.

"You're coming with us," Swenson said, grabbing one arm as Draper took hold of the other. "Don't yell or make a fuss or so help me you'll wish you hadn't."

Before he knew what was happening, Randy was in the barber chair, a smock tied around his neck.

"If you don't want your scalp tore up, you better not make any sudden moves," Swenson advised, turning on the clippers.

"He better not make any moves at all," Draper said, brandishing one of Swenson's straight razors.

"Why are you doing this?" was all Randy managed to say. Swenson told him to shut the hell up, and he obliged.

Five minutes later Randy hardly recognized himself. He easily could have belonged to one of the two groups he most despised: short-haired businessmen and right-wing military types. He almost would have rather had his throat cut.

"No charge," Swenson said, freeing him from the smock. "I must say your looks have improved considerable."

Randy stared with horror at his shorn image in the mirror. "Why'd you do that to me?" he asked. "Why?"

"Nothing personal, son. You needed a haircut and we wanted to make sure you got one."

Randy headed for the door, but before he got there

he swung around. "There ought to be a skull and crossbones at the edge of town instead of that ridiculous Welcome-to-Chockoyotte sign," he said, hardly able to hold back his tears. "People should be warned not to stop here or they'll get abused by ... by the goddamn niggers and rednecks. You know something? This town sucks. It really does. It ought to be bombed off the face of the fucking earth!"

COURSE OF DISTINCTION (1982)

I'm no Charlie Sifford, Pete Brown, Lee Elder, or Calvin Peete—I couldn't hold a candle to the likes of them. But there is one thing I did before any other black golfer, professional or otherwise, and that includes Webster Jenkins, chief surgeon at the county hospital. Everybody thinks Webster broke the color barrier at Chockoyotte Country Club, but they're mistaken. He might've been the first black to play a round of golf out here, but the first to *complete* a round was me, Moses Bibby, former caddie and present greenskeeper. It might not have been pretty how I did it—in installments and at odd hours—but it got done, and Webster was still slicing up cadavers at Bowman Gray.

I always did love this course, ever since I was a kid and my next older brother talked me into signing up as a caddie. The trees are mature and stately and the fairways lush and green. Even the traps are appealing, full of white sand that glints in the sun like sugar, not that muddy-looking stuff they use at the course I play near Emporia. Each hole is unique and they all have character, nine jewels set in a precious crown. But the first and the last are the best. They're the ones I'll recall when I'm in the old folks home gumming my food and trying to remember my kids' names.

Normally when the last golfers finish in the evening, there's still some daylight left, enough to get in two or three holes if you play fast and can tolerate the mosquitoes. Sometimes when we were feeling brave, or just couldn't stand it anymore, my brother and me—and later just me—would walk down the road toward the railroad tracks like we were heading home for the night, and when we got past where folks could see us, we'd sneak back onto the course and play a hole or two, using clubs we'd stashed in the woods. The only problem was we could never under any circumstance play number one or number nine. Those holes are in full view of the clubhouse, and if the pro ever got wind of what we were doing, our caddying days would be over.

Number one is a 443-yard par four dogleg left with a green tucked into a stand of white pines and guarded in front by a ditch. Your drive has to be long and straight or you can forget about getting home in two. Your second shot has to be even better, just the right distance and direction or you'll wind up in the ditch or the trees. That hole has ruined many a golfer's day before it hardly got started.

Number nine is a slightly uphill 258-yard par four

with a fairway so narrow you can spit across it. The left side slopes into a ravine and the right is hemmed in by the access road to the clubhouse, which is out of bounds. If you catch your drive just right, you can be putting for an eagle. But if you hook the ball or slice it, you're in jail, doomed to a bogey or worse. It's a great finishing hole, something to look forward to at the end of each round. For years I dreamed of playing it as a homesick soldier might yearn for the woman he left behind.

It was Bernice Barnes, the mayor's wife, who finally gave me my one-time pass to come home.

There she is now with her friend Tillie following their drives up the fifth fairway, my reason for all this reminiscing in the first place. I pull the tractor and mowing equipment over to the rough and cut the motor, deciding to take a smoke break while they play through. They're almost past when my mouth opens in spite of myself and I call out: "Mornin', Miz Barnes. Miz Storch. Haven't run across any vipers today, have you?"

Tillie's smile tells me she'd like nothing better than to find a nest of water moccasins and have me staked out in the middle. Or maybe squeezed to a slow death by a giant boa constrictor ...

"No, Moses. No snakes today. But if we see one, we'll be sure to call you."

Bernice pretends to ignore me, but I know she hasn't succeeded when she shanks her next shot into the sixth fairway and stands there glaring after it. The only reason she keeps from cussing is because she doesn't want to give me the satisfaction.

"Even Webster hits 'em better than that," I tease, knowing I better watch my tongue. "And he's so busy being a white man he rarely works on his game."

She gives me a little smile of forbearance. "Ever since Dr. Jenkins started playing this course, you haven't been yourself, Moses. Seems like you'd be happy for him ... and for your race."

I chew on that one a while, wishing I could spit it back at her. "I think you're standing too far from the ball," I finally say, determined to keep my cool. "You're also dipping your left shoulder too much on the take-away."

"You know, that's exactly what the new pro told me at my last lesson. I'll try to pay more attention to it. Have a nice day, Moses. And thanks for the advice."

She's right, of course. I did change after Webster started playing out here. To tell the truth, I never did like the guy. He was two years ahead of me at Ralph Bunche and we played on some of the same athletic teams. In football he was our quarterback, and whenever we won, it was always because he did this and he did that, regardless of who the real stars happened to be. When we lost, he usually blamed it on somebody else or on the team as a whole. He played first base on our baseball team. I'll never forget one particular grounder that squirted through his legs. In the dugout he claimed he lost it in his shadow. When I reminded him the sun wasn't even out at the time, he threw a punch at me and Coach had to pull us apart.

But there's more to it than Webster. You see that rain shelter over there between the two fairways? That's where it all started, one overcast spring morning quite a few years ago ...

I was mowing the fifth fairway when all of a sudden the sky turned black. I didn't pay much attention until I finally heard the thunder over the tractor's motor. When rain drops began pinging off the hood, I knew I couldn't get back to the clubhouse in time, so I headed for that shed, getting there just as Bernice and Tillie did, hightailing it from the fourth green. All three of us were soaked. Lightning crackled overhead and thunder crashed, the rain pounding the tin roof like stones.

"Storm sure came up fast," I said.

They ignored me and sat down on the bench farthest from the entrance.

"Mess up a good round for either of you?" I asked.

Bernice shook her head. "Nobody would've mistaken me for Nancy Lopez."

"Me neither. That's a vicious-looking sky, Bernie. Looks like we're stuck here a while."

I took out my smokes and offered them one, but they declined and began chatting about things that didn't remotely pertain to me. After a while I resigned myself to smoking in silence.

I'd just flipped the cigarette butt into the rain when my mind registered something I'd glimpsed a few seconds earlier, something out of the ordinary I'd seen but not really seen. I looked again and there it was, under the bench where the women were sitting, a spotted coil, motionless in the dirt except for an occasional flicking of tongue.

"Ladies, I'd like you to stick your feet out real slow and fold your legs up under you."

"What the hell is he talking about?" Tillie said, and

they both looked at me like I'd just escaped from Dix Hill.

I leaned over and casually selected a club from one of their bags, a short iron because I could wield it better.

"Just do like I say and do it slow and easy." I didn't want to scare them for fear they'd make a sudden movement.

"Why're you so interested in our legs?" Bernice asked and started swinging hers back and forth.

The snake struck her and she screamed.

"Jump away!" I yelled. "It's a copperhead!"

I flung aside the bench and gave the snake a whack just as it was coiling to strike again, dazing it enough so I could grab it by the tail and snap it against the shed. Then I tossed it out in the rain where it writhed a little before lying still. Lightning snicked, exploding into nearby pines. A limb tumbled down, crashing against the ground.

"It bit me, Tillie. That damn snake bit me. I need to get to the hospital."

Tillie's mouth was working but no words were coming out. "I ... I know it," she finally said and helped her friend to the bench I'd been occupying. "But the storm, Bernie. We could get killed by lightning."

"For God's sake, Tillie. A snake just bit me, a poisonous snake! I've got to see a doctor before it's too late."

When I suggested I cut her leg with my pocket knife and suck out the poison, they looked at me like I wasn't just a typical Dix Hill escapee but the bull goose loony himself.

"A pocket knife?" Tillie said. "A dirty pocket knife?"

"I'll sterilize it as best I can."

I took out my knife, lit a match, and held it under the blade, careful not to let the flame get high enough to leave a soot deposit. When the match burned down, I lit another and then a third and a fourth, each time letting the tip of the flame lick at the blade. All the while the women watched me like I was a witchdoctor in a Tarzan movie.

"I don't know," Bernice said. "I don't know if I want you cutting me with that."

"It's sharp," I said. "And it's clean now. You won't get infected."

Lightning cracked across the sky like a long white whip, snapping out thunder. The ground shook and the shed rattled.

"Better let him do it, Bernie. You can't just sit here. And God knows we can't go out in this storm."

"All right," she finally said. "But he damn well better know what he's doing."

I sat down in front of her and, after pinching the flesh just above the fang marks, made a little X. She yelled both times I cut. Then she asked Tillie to suck out the poison.

"No offense. I'd just rather she did it."

Tillie's eyes resembled a cat's at a fireworks display. She looked so pale I thought I might have to expand my medical practice.

"I can't. Believe me I would if I could, Bernie. I just can't."

So ole black lips was finally authorized to suck out the poison. It tasted like sour milk and sweat as I spat it on the ground.

"You sure this'll work?" Bernice asked while I was tying my handkerchief as a tourniquet just below her knee. "I'm going to be all right, aren't I? It hurts like hell."

I nodded. "I don't think you got anything to worry about. After the storm lets up, we'll get you back to the clubhouse. Mr. Tolbert'll have somebody drive you to the hospital where they can check you out. Takes copperhead poison a while to work if you don't exert yourself."

When the storm finally passed, I offered to carry her to the tractor, but she told me she'd rather walk. After I explained how even a small amount of exercise could pump any venom I might've missed into her bloodstream, she agreed to be carried, but she kept one arm against my shoulder, more as a brace against my getting any closer than a means to hold on.

Fifteen minutes later when I set her down in a chair on the clubhouse veranda, she opened her purse and handed me a twenty-dollar bill.

"No need," I said.

"Take it. You earned it. You might've saved my life."

"No thanks. I don't take money for doing somebody a favor."

"Then let me give you a present. There must be something you'd like to have ... within reason, of course. Name it."

Suddenly it occurred to me there really was

something she might be able to give me. It probably wasn't within what she'd call reason, but I wanted it so bad I went ahead and asked.

"I'd like to play number one and number nine," I said.

"What?" She looked at me the same way she did when I volunteered to cut her leg with my knife.

"I don't mean right now or during regular hours. I'd just like to play those two holes sometime, maybe early one morning when nobody else is around. I thought you might be able to arrange something with Mr. Tolbert. If you can't, that's OK. I'll understand."

"I'll think about it," she said.

Three days later Roy Tolbert, the club pro, drove an electric cart out to the third green where I was relocating the cup.

"Your tee time is five o'clock tomorrow morning," he said. "You'll have until five-thirty at the absolute latest to finish both holes. Start with number one so you can end up back at the clubhouse. I don't think anybody'll be out that early, but if somebody does show up, take your clubs and head for the woods or the ravine. And don't you ever pull a stunt like this again, Moses, or so help me I'll fire you so fast you'll think you were the one got snake bit. Is that understood?"

I nodded.

"One other thing. I've never actually seen you doing it, but I've heard rumors you occasionally play some of those other holes. That's going to have to stop. If it doesn't, I'll have to fire you for that too."

That night I had a hard time falling asleep, partly because it took me a while to figure out my scores on the other seven holes. Over the years I'd birdied all of them except number seven, a long uphill par three with a two-tiered green, but what I needed to know was exactly what I did on each of those holes the last time I played it. Come morning I wanted to be able to post a legitimate nine-hole score, if only in my head.

My drive on number one was exactly what I'd hoped for, long and on the right side of the fairway. I didn't get quite all of my second shot, just enough to get it over the ditch. Because of the dew on the green, I chipped harder than I normally would, too hard it turned out because the ball rolled about nine feet past the cup. Then I putted too easy. At least I thought I did because the ball looked for all the world like it was going to stop before it reached the hole. It hovered on the lip for a few seconds and finally dropped in.

On number nine I pushed my drive and ended up across the road just short of green high. Disgusted with myself, I teed up again, strengthened my grip a tad, and tried to put everything out of my mind except swinging smooth and strong and finishing with a high follow-through. It worked. The ball soared straight toward the green, exactly the way I'd envisioned it the thousand or so times I'd played the hole in my mind. It landed about thirty feet short of the green, bounded between the traps and through the fringe, and rolled to within eight feet of the cup.

As luck would have it, my putt lipped out and I had to settle for a bogey five.

A few weeks after Webster started playing out here, I was mowing number eight when he and one of the white doctors that sponsor him played through. I waved as they passed, but they didn't see me—or didn't want to. After they putted out, I followed them over toward number nine and watched them tee off. Webster pushed his drive across the road into the number one fairway. The other doctor did the same thing.

"Let's play 'em where they lay," Webster said. "It's ridiculous to be penalized for shots like that. They'd be decent drives on any other hole."

The white doctor agreed. They both pitched on the green, two putted, and congratulated themselves on their pars.

When Webster came out of the clubhouse after taking his shower, I was waiting. I knew what I was about to do was dumb, that I should just let it go, chalk it up as something I had no control over, like lightning or a good shot that caroms off a rock or a root and skips into the rough. But I just couldn't let him get away with it.

"Don't think for a minute you and Ben Casey over there got pars on number nine," I said as calmly as I could, my voice shaking. "You should've teed up again or played your second shot from where the ball went out of bounds. Either way you needed to take a penalty stroke."

"Nigger, I don't believe we've met," Webster said and tried to push past me to his car. "What say we keep it that way."

I turned him around with my left hand and hit him once with my right, a quick jab to the nose that snapped his head back and dropped him to the pavement like a sack of feed.

I expected to get fired. Surprisingly enough Roy Tolbert never mentioned the incident, at least not until years later. In fact, he didn't bring it up until his last day at the course, right before he left to become the assistant pro at the Carolina Country Club in Raleigh.

"Moses, did you ever wonder how you managed to keep your job after that little altercation with Dr. Jenkins?"

"I figured he decided not to report me."

"Oh, he reported you all right." He held his thumb and index finger about a quarter inch apart. "And I came within this far of firing you."

"Why didn't you?"

We were standing between the veranda and the putting green, and he turned and gazed out over the course, his eyes taking on a far-away look. "You remember that morning you played number one and number nine?"

"Just like yesterday. I was even par when I teed off."

"When you teed off? I don't understand."

"That's what I shot the last time I played those other seven holes. It was over a span of years, so it took me a while figuring out exactly what my scores were. I birdied both par fives, double bogied number seven, and parred the rest."

"What happened on seven?"

"I hooked a 3-iron into the woods and hit a tree when I chipped out."

"Seven is a bear, Moses. Anyway, after you got back to the clubhouse, I asked how you did on one and nine. The truth is I really didn't need to ask. I already knew. I saw you roll in that knee knocker on one and …"

"You were in the woods spying on me?"

He chuckled. "I was spying on you but not from the woods. I brought my binoculars that morning. By the way, number nine is one of my all-time favorite holes. After you missed that putt, I found myself quite interested in how you'd score the hole. I knew it would hurt like hell for a golfer of your ability not to get at least a par the one chance you had to play it. Considering the circumstances, most folks would've taken a mulligan, which I thought you were doing when you hit your second drive. Then they'd claim a birdie and not give it a second thought. Like Dr. Jenkins gave himself a par that day you tried to rearrange his face."

"So you knew why I hit him. He admitted cheating."

"No, it never occurred to him he'd done anything wrong. But the more he talked the more I found myself sympathizing with you. The doctors he plays with expected me to fire you, as did quite a few other members. I took a considerable amount of heat before the incident finally died down."

"I appreciate that," I said.

"My pleasure." He stuck out his hand. "You and this course are a lot alike, Moses. You're both tough old sons of bitches with a lot of character. It wouldn't have been right to separate the two of you."

ELLIE AND BUS (1986)

When I wake up, I don't know where I am. Not a clue as they say on TV. Like the time I ran off and got lost in the woods, had to wait for the staff to come rescue me. That was before Bus started working at Ridge Road. I haven't run off since.

They say that a lot lately, the staff does. Poor Ellie she doesn't have a clue. They're right most of the time. Like now when all I know for sure is my stomach hurts, deep down in the pit where my supper must've settled. This bed is harder than the one I usually sleep on. The room looks different too, the walls all white, the window in the wrong place. There's no Kermit the Frog sitting on the dresser. No sweet old Frosty dog smiling at me from inside his picture.

I think of Bus, see him waltzing in and wishing me a good morning like he used to, asking what I want for breakfast. Like I really have a choice. Pancakes and sausage, I tried to tell him once, but it just comes out the way my words always do, all run together like the inside of a rotten egg.

The door opens and somebody comes in, a woman I've never seen before. She smiles at me, says she's a nurse, then takes my temperature and blood pressure. I decide I'm in a hospital, but I don't know why until a man wearing a rubber necklace hikes up my gown and starts poking around my private place. When I realize his necklace is one of those things doctors listen to you with, I figure they brought me in to check the seed Bus planted down there.

"Everything looks fine, Ellie," he tells me and pats my hand. "You'll probably be sore for a few days, but after a week or so you shouldn't be any the worse for wear."

After he leaves I think of Bus, wonder why he's staying gone so long.

"I'm Mike Fergus, Mr. Radcliff," the lawyer says as he enters the small room where I've been sitting the past half hour. He's wearing a gray pinstripe suit and looks young enough to be my son, not that I'll ever have one or a daughter either. "Court lasted longer than usual this morning."

"No problem," I tell him as we shake hands. "It's not like I'm in a hurry to get somewhere. This shouldn't take long anyway. I'm pleading guilty."

He sits down across the table, opens his briefcase, and takes out an official-looking sheet of paper. "From what I know so far, I think you'll have a better chance if we go to trial."

I shake my head. "It'd be a waste of everybody's time. I did what they said I did. I'll take whatever punishment the judge gives me."

"Well, a lot will depend on the circumstances. Without knowing exactly what they are, I'd say you're looking at anywhere from one to fifteen years."

"Fifteen years doesn't seem unreasonable for what I did to Ellie."

He gives me a strange look, like I've lost most of my marbles, maybe even come from a different planet. "How long did you work at Ridge Road Group Home before the ... uh, incident, Mr. Radcliff?"

"Might as well call me Bus," I tell him. "Everybody else does."

"Short for Buster?"

"Nope." I manage a smile, probably my first in over a month. "When I was in the third grade, I got caught in the back door of a school bus. At least part of me did. The rest dangled outside until the darn thing stopped to let out the next batch of kids."

He chuckles in a nervous sort of way, like he might find what I said funny under different circumstances but he's too preoccupied with the here and now to fully appreciate it.

"To answer your question, I was at Ridge Road almost three years. It was my first group home job ... and my last. Not that I didn't like the work. Nobody in their right mind would hire me again after what I did."

He unbuttons his shirt collar and loosens his tie, doesn't look quite as uptight. "What kind of work did you do before you hired on at Ridge Road, Bus?"

"Worked at the paper mill a while, then at Jamison

Valve. A few years ago I started my own handyman business. Turned out I couldn't make enough to live on, so I took a part time job at the group home to help make ends meet."

"So you've actually been working two jobs the last few years?"

I nod. "Didn't keep me out of trouble, did it?"

He gives me a puny smile and jots something on the paper. "I see you had a heart attack a while back. That must've slowed you down a bit."

"A couple of weeks is all. The doctor said it was mild as those things go."

"I'm sure you know even a mild heart attack can't be taken lightly," he tells me, then looks down at the sheet of paper. "According to the prosecutor, you raped a retarded client at the group home. Is that an accurate assessment of what happened?"

"I'm not sure I'd call it rape. But that's probably close enough for legal purposes."

"What would you call it, Bus?" he asks, not unkindly.

I think about that a while. "Don't really know," I finally tell him. "I do know what I did was wrong and I definitely shouldn't have done it. A decent man wouldn't take advantage of Ellie the way I did."

He nods, lets my answer sink in. "By any chance was she a willing participant?"

"She didn't put up a struggle, but that's because she trusted me."

"Did she ever come on to you in any way, say or do anything that might be considered seductive?"

"Not once."

"It wouldn't have to be something obvious—a touch here, a flirtatious smile there, anything that might make a reasonable person think she was ... well, hot to trot."

I shake my head. "Ellie is brain damaged, Mr. Fergus. What happened to her was all my doing."

He glances down at his sheet. "It says here you live at the Meadows Trailer Court between Chockoyotte and Roanoke Falls and that you're single. Have you ever been married?"

"Nope. Never have."

"Do you have a girlfriend?"

"Not at the moment." I pause, look down at my hands. "To tell the truth, I haven't had one for a long time."

"How long?"

"Years ... a lot of years. I'm not gay, though. Sometimes I almost wish I was. Things might've been easier."

"How do you mean?"

I stare at the wall, see dust mice where the molding meets the floor. "I'd rather not go into that if you don't mind. It really doesn't have anything to do with why either one of us is here."

"Why don't you let me decide that?" He's like a bulldog now, unwilling to give up the bone I tossed him by mistake.

"It's old news I'd like to forget. I shouldn't have brought it up."

"At least tell me whether you had a sexual relationship with this girlfriend."

I bite my lower lip. "I don't think that's anybody's business but mine ... and hers."

"Listen, Bus. You've been accused of committing a serious sex crime. Whoever passes sentence on you will want to know your sexual history. If your lawyer doesn't cover it to the judge's satisfaction, he'll most likely ask you to cover it."

"If the judge wants to know about my sex life, I'll tell him. But unless and until he asks, I don't want to talk about it. I'm not trying to be hard to get along with, Mr. Fergus. I just don't want to pick at old scabs unless I have to."

He nods, scribbles a few more notes, then slides the sheet of paper back in his briefcase. "There's one thing you need to know before we go any further. I haven't been a lawyer very long, and I've never had a case even remotely resembling yours. If it's not handled right, it could turn out disastrous for you. A while ago I said you're probably looking at one to fifteen years, but depending on who the judge happens to be and how you're represented, you could get a lot more. Life isn't out of the question if you're unfortunate enough to draw George Courtright, who's from the old, old school when it comes to anything resembling rape."

"Are you telling me you don't want me for a client?"

He shakes his head. "I'm telling you it would be in your best interest to request another lawyer. They'll give you one if you ask. Just say you don't think someone with my lack of experience is capable of providing you the best defense, which is true."

"I don't want another lawyer," I tell him. "You turned out exactly the way I hoped you would."

He gives me a puzzled look. "Why do you say that?"

"You're not an asshole like I thought you'd be."

The leaves on the pecan tree outside my window tell me a breeze is stirring. I wait for it to sift through the screen but it never does. I turn over for the umpteenth time, feel my nightgown sticking to my back. I lay there in my sweat, staring at the man in the moon, wondering if he's hot as I am.

Bus once told me if I'm having trouble sleeping I should think about something nice, something that gives me pleasure. That would be him, of course, and I think of the night he saved me from the red-eyed monster climbing over my window sill.

Take it easy, he tells me. I'm right here. He strokes my forehead and speaks soft words until the monster turns into a silly-looking white rabbit and hightails it out of there. You were having a bad dream, Ellie. A nightmare actually. That's what they're called when they're extra scary.

He pats my shoulder, tells me everything's going to be all right. He starts to leave, tells me to sleep tight.

Don't go, Bus, I say. God knows what the words sound like, but he seems to understand and comes back and sits down on the edge of the bed.

I'll stay a few more minutes, Ellie. You try to go back to sleep.

Hoping he won't mind, I take his hand and place it on my chest right where my heart should be. Then I close my eyes and settle into the warm feeling of Bus being there next to me.

"I have some questions for you, Mr. Radcliff," the

judge says, a tall, swarthy individual with a neatly trimmed beard. "Before I ask them, though, I'd like to commend Mr. Fergus on his presentation. In spite of the fact that you committed a crime you yourself describe as indefensible, he managed to present you in something of a favorable light. Apparently you're an honest, hardworking man, and from all indications you feel considerable remorse for what you did."

"I do."

He fixes me with a stare I have no idea how to interpret. "I'm just curious as to why you did it. Having sex with a severely retarded woman under your care seems so out of character ... unless there was something going on quite apart from a desire to satisfy your animal urges." He pauses, seems to be sizing me up. "Do you think your heart attack might have had something to do with it?"

I give him a puzzled look. "No, sir. To tell the truth, I never gave that a thought."

"I'll get right to the point, Mr. Radcliff. Was Ellie Schmidt your first sexual experience?"

I look away, past the court stenographer and the empty jury box. My gaze finally comes to rest on the wall clock. The second hand moves a quarter way round the face before I reply. "I was with a hooker one time in Tennessee."

"How old were you then?"

"I'd just turned twenty-one."

"That's a long time ago, Mr. Radcliff. Have you had sexual relations with anyone between the time you had relations with this prostitute and the time you impregnated Ellie?"

I look at my hands, see nails bitten down to the quick. I feel like I'm inside an old snow globe, part of a winter scene. The judge has turned it upside down and is staring at it, waiting for the snow to settle so he can tell exactly who or what is standing there in the cold. "I didn't have relations with her," I tell him. "I couldn't. I was too scared."

He nods, then gives the globe another shake, just hard enough to set the flakes in motion again. "Were there other women in your life between the prostitute and Ellie Schmidt?"

I stare at the clock, see the second hand move from the two to the five. From the corner of my eye I can see Marlene Parker glaring at me from the nearly empty spectators' gallery. "Yes, sir. There was one."

"Tell me about her."

I look at my hands again, feel pools of wet collecting in the corners of my eyes. "She was everything a man could ask for," I say. "Smart, good looking, had a great personality, even enjoyed the same things I did. She was the love of my life ... or could've been."

"What happened, Mr. Radcliff?"

This time I stare at the floor, try to focus on how grubby my shoes look compared to my lawyer's. "She was so special it scared me," I say, my voice trembling. "Scared me so bad that every time I tried to make love to her, I'd ... I'd be limp as a dishrag."

By the time Mike leads me out of the courtroom, I can't see a thing because of my damn tears.

"He got what!" I hear big Mary Lou roar. She's in the kitchen, stuffing her face with the cookies she made for us clients. They're not chocolate chip so I don't really mind.

"Probation," Giles tells her. He's been talking on the phone and just hung up. "Marlene was there when the judge pronounced sentence. Said it made her want to vomit."

"Well, it does me too. How can Bus Radcliff get off that easy after what he did? I figured they'd lock him up and throw away the key."

Hearing Bus's name, I move closer. Mary Lou slips another sugar cookie in her mouth. She makes almost two of Giles, who was hired to fill in until Bus comes back.

"Me too. He must've had a super slick lawyer, though I wouldn't have thought F. Lee Bailey himself could've got him probation."

"Football!" Tyrone yells from the living room. "Hockey? Wanna go play hockey?"

"Shut the fuck up," Weezie tells him from the sofa. Normally she sits there in a daze and never says a word, but her favorite soap opera is on TV. "You wouldn't know a football from a goddamn hockey puck."

"Watch your mouth, Weezie," Mary Lou calls but not in a mean way. "Tyrone's just being Tyrone."

Giles takes one of the sugar cookies and pops it in his mouth. "What was Bus like, Mary Lou? I never had the pleasure of meeting the dude."

"Good question." She pours herself a glass of Kool-Aid. There's never enough sugar in it so I don't mind. "Actually I kind of liked him until I found out what he did to Ellie. He was friendly enough and pulled his end of the load, wasn't a slacker like some of the turkeys come through here."

"Hope you're not including me in that bunch."

She smiles. "No, not you, Giles. Though it would be nice if you volunteered a little more often to change Tyrone's shitty pants. Bus never shied away from shit, I'll give him that. And he was good with the clients, had a way of getting them to do what he wanted. Even Carl behaved when Bus was on duty. He's the autistic guy they moved to another group home to make room for Weezie."

"Was Bus mean to the clients?"

"No, he wasn't. He never hit anyone, never even raised his voice that I recall."

"How'd he manage to get Ellie off by herself long enough to get her pregnant? I mean there's a state law prohibiting male staff from being alone with a female client. Marlene made me memorize the damn thing before she hired me."

"It happened on the night shift when a female staffer was sleeping on the job, literally. Marlene fired her the same day Bus got arrested."

The first thing I do when I get back to the trailer is head for the kitchen, hoping the fridge still works and there's at least one beer inside. Turns out there's three, all the perfect temperature. I pop the cap on one, take a long pull. Somehow it just doesn't taste as good as it should.

The same can be said of my freedom. I know I ought to be happy about the way things turned out. Not having to spend time in prison where I'd have to worry about some guy doing to me what I did to Ellie is definitely something to be thankful for. And I am thankful. But I'd be lying if I said I'm happy. How could I be, knowing I forced myself on a retarded woman? A man can't get much lower than that.

Back in the living room I rummage through my CDs until I find the one with "Take It Easy," my favorite song. I slip it in the CD player and turn it on, then sit on the sofa and prop my feet up on the coffee table. When the Eagles get to the refrain, I join them, almost feeling like one of the group. Those boys sure do know how to sing.

When the song is over, I play it again, this time joining in at the beginning. "There's a girl, my Lord, in a flatbed Ford, slowing down to take a look at me," I belt out, then realize how ridiculous it is for me, of all people, to be singing those words. I'm about as far from resembling that guy on the corner in Winslow, Arizona as a person can get.

I think of Sandra, wonder what kind of man she ended up marrying, what kind of family she's got. At least I was the one to finally call it quits. I didn't hang on until she was forced to cut me loose …

"Take it easy," the Eagles sing. "Don't let the sound of your own wheels drive you crazy."

I think of Ellie, see her sitting between Tyrone and Weezie at the dining room table, waiting for me to serve the evening meal. What an appetite that girl had, and yet there wasn't an ounce of fat on her. After dinner I always read them a few pages from one of the books I kept from my childhood— *Longlegs the Heron*, *The Real Mother Goose*, *The Wind in the Willows*, *Uncle Wiggily's Airship*. Sometimes Tyrone and

Weezie would listen, and sometimes they'd drift off to their rooms or watch TV with the other staffer. But Ellie was always there next to me on the sofa, taking in every word.

I hope to God I didn't do her any permanent damage.

I'm staring out the window at tracks in the powder somebody dumped all over the yard when I see a car pull in the driveway. It's Marlene and I'm disappointed. I was hoping this would be the night Bus finally came back.

I look at the tracks. I'm pretty sure they're made by deer, and I think of the morning Bus woke me ahead of the others and led me by the hand to this same window.

Take a look out there, Ellie, he whispers. Ever see such a sight?

At first I don't know what he's talking about, but then I see them, two tan critters easing across the yard like smoke. The one in front has bones sticking out of his head, antlers I later learn when Bus shows me his picture in a magazine.

Now look over there, just to the left of that spruce.

I follow his finger until I see two little spotted guys, their scrawny bods looking silly on top of stovepipe legs. One sniffs the other's butt and gets chased around the spruce for his trouble.

Those are fawns, Bus tells me. The bigger ones are the mom and dad.

I hear the front door open. Marlene steps inside, stomping her feet on the mat and shaking white powder off her coat.

"Hello, Ellie," she says when she notices me. "Quite a winter wonderland out there, isn't it? Hello, Tyrone, Weezie. Anything good on TV?" She takes off her boots, tosses them in the closet with her coat. "Tomorrow we'll bundle you guys up and take you for a walk. Think you'll like that?"

"Football!" Tyrone responds. "Wanna go play hockey?"

"Not tonight, Ty." She goes in the kitchen where Mary Lou is finishing up the dishes. "Sorry I'm late. Just as I was getting ready to leave I got a call that stopped me in my tracks. Bus Radcliff died this afternoon."

"You're kidding!" Mary Lou says, turning off the water. She dries her hands and waddles over to the dining room table where Marlene has already sat down. "What happened?"

"Apparently he was shoveling snow and had a heart attack. He didn't get to enjoy his probation very long, did he?"

"Here I thought that guy was leading a charmed life. Just goes to show you, I guess. You never know who or when the grim reaper's gonna strike."

Marlene gives a snort. "I hate to speak ill of the dead, but in Bus's case I'm going to make an exception. The way I see it, the grim reaper didn't claim that scumbag. It was the angel of justice."

"Can't argue with that. I still can't believe a judge let him off the hook after what he did."

"That judge is an irresponsible jackass. I never told you, Mary Lou, but Bus Radcliff came within a hair's breadth of closing down this group home … and all because he couldn't keep his weasel in his pants. I refuse to attend his funeral. I hope none of the staff goes."

"I doubt anyone will. It's hard to pay last respects to somebody you didn't respect in the first place."

I'm running toward them now, screaming, the only sound I can make that comes out saying what I mean it to. I slam my fist against the side of Marlene's head, then start in on Mary Lou. I go from one to the other until they wrestle me down and pin me to the floor.

"Stop it, Ellie!" Marlene yells and slaps me twice, hard. "Stop it right now!"

"What's gotten into her?" Mary Lou says. "I've never seen her so out of control."

"Can you hold her down long enough for me to call for help?"

"I think so. But please hurry."

I keep on thrashing and screaming until somebody I've never seen before jabs a needle in my arm. I'm like a clock that's been wound too tight, my hands flying all over the place. Gradually I slow down, keep on slowing until time finally catches up, then scoots on ahead.

As I drift off to sleep, I hear Bus's voice. He's sitting next to me on the sofa, reading from *The Wind in the Willows*.

ONCE IN A GREAT WHILE (1996)

Walter Hux had never felt more depressed in his life. It wasn't that he missed the activity of the last three days—a steady stream of visitors to the farm, his son-in-law twice requiring his assistance in Norlina to help with supplies, his daughter volunteering his services to look at one neighbor's cow, another's lethargic horse, a third's sluggish pig. Even his grandchildren had gotten into the act, hauling him around to see this friend's hamster, that one's litter of kittens, another's pet rabbit—as though a veterinarian of over forty years needed contact with animals every waking minute.

"Next time you invite me for a weekend get-together, you might try holding the festivities at Grand Central Station," he had told his daughter as he prepared to leave, trying to hide his despondency behind a mask of humor. "It won't be nearly as hectic."

His daughter had smiled. "I know how unhappy you've been, Dad. I was hoping all the activity would lift your spirits."

"It did, Brenda," he lied. "I feel better now than before I came."

"You'll feel even better soon," she said and gave him a strong goodbye hug. "Remember what Mom used to say—time heals all wounds."

Not this one, he wanted to tell her, disappointed that Brenda hadn't grasped the enormity of the incident or the intensity of his reaction to it. How could she? She had her own family to think about, her own life to lead. It's not like she had been there to witness it ... or could do anything about it.

Doug Courtright had been there, though, and being the sheriff as well as a friend he could and should have done something. Doug had watched him pull back the blood-soaked blanket, had seen the result of the atrocity first hand. "What kind of warped son of a bitch would do that?" he had muttered before turning away.

"Who else but Ned Copeland ... in retaliation for my part in closing down his puppy mill?"

The sheriff nodded. "You're probably right. He waited just long enough so it wouldn't be obvious."

"That puppy was still alive when I found him, Doug. He'd been skinned and left on a cold concrete slab. Can you imagine the suffering? You can't let Copeland get away with that."

"I'll do what I can, Walt. But Ned's a shrewd one. He's probably covered his tracks."

"Aren't you going to arrest him?"

"I will if I can come up with evidence linking him to the crime."

"What if you can't?"

"It'll depend on how he reacts when I question him. If he says something incriminating, I'll lock him up. But if he denies everything and doesn't slip up in the process, there's not much I can do."

A week went by and the sheriff acknowledged that he was no closer to arresting Ned Copeland than on the day Dr. Hux reported the crime. "I haven't found a soul who saw anything suspicious at Ned's place or your clinic. I haven't even found anybody who lost, sold, or gave away a German shepherd puppy."

"Why don't you lock him up anyway? You know as well as I do he's guilty."

"What I know and what I can prove are two different things. Without actual evidence a judge will throw out the case. There are other possibilities, Walt. Someone you had a run-in with years ago could've done it. So could a person you don't even know, some sicko who gets his kicks from doing things twisted and sadistic."

"But why leave the pup on the clinic porch unless the act was directed at me?"

"Somebody might've found it and wanted to help but was scared you'd think he or she was the person responsible."

"Bullshit! It didn't happen that way and you know it."

"Maybe, but that's a reasonable-enough explanation if you're looking at it from the outside, which a judge or a jury will do. They won't convict just because Ned has a motive and a bad reputation. Sure, I'm convinced he's guilty. I knew him in his younger days when he did a lot of things decent people don't do. He was mean then and he hasn't mellowed with age. I know how much this bothers you, Walt, but my hands are tied. Like I told you the other day, this kind of crime is almost impossible to prosecute. You need a witness or a confession, and so far I haven't been able to come up with either."

"Then I'll just have to take care of things myself."

"Oh? What exactly have you got in mind?"

"You'll see."

That evening Dr. Hux drove out past the gut bridge to a frame house some two miles east of Chockoyotte. He parked behind a ten-year-old white Cadillac convertible in immaculate condition. As he got out of his car, he heard the periodic pop of what sounded like a .22 rifle, and he walked around to the familiar backyard and found Ned Copeland taking target practice at tin cans atop wooden posts, all that remained of what had once been a large dog pen.

"Well, well, would you look who's here," Copeland said, a wiry man with a ruddy face and white hair pulled back in a ponytail. "You paying a social call, Doc, or checking to see if I'm still in the puppy business?"

"I'm here to find out if you're responsible for the one left on my clinic porch."

"Couldn't have been me. Hasn't been a pup around here since you and Courtright closed me down."

"The one I'm talking about was skinned alive."

"You don't say. Well, I wouldn't know anything about that."

"I think you do. I think you know plenty."

Copeland raised the rifle to his shoulder and squeezed the trigger, sending a can toppling to the ground. "If I was the one responsible, I'd be a fool to say so, now wouldn't I? If you think it was me, fine. Maybe next time you'll think twice before bringing somebody up on a trumped-up charge." In a quick fluid motion he cocked the rifle and fired. Another can dropped to the ground. "Deer season's just around the corner, Doc. You oughta buy yourself a gun and try being a real man for a change. Hunting's a lot more wholesome than minding other people's business."

"Funny you'd say that. As a matter of fact, I am going to buy a gun. But it's not deer I plan to shoot."

"Oh? What then?"

"You."

Copeland's eyes widened. "Me? Because of what happened to that pup?"

"You're going to answer for that, one way or another. Either you confess and accept whatever punishment the court gives you, or I'll administer the punishment I think you deserve."

The incredulity on Copeland's face turned to amusement. "You expect me to confess because of a dumb-ass threat like that?"

"I don't expect anything. I'm just telling you what will happen if you don't turn yourself in."

"Don't you know it's against the law to go around threatening people, Doc? I could have *you* arrested."

"Cruelty to animals is against the law too, but that didn't stop you. You're going to pay for what you did. Either the court will punish you or I will. You've got exactly one week to decide which it's going to be."

Copeland guffawed. "You wouldn't know which end of a gun to aim. And if you ever did figure it out, you wouldn't have the balls to pull the trigger. If you think you can bluff a confession out of Ned Copeland, you're crazier than a goddamn loon."

"I'm not bluffing," Dr. Hux said, then turned and walked away. Raucous laughter followed him all the way to his car.

The following afternoon Doug Courtright stopped by the veterinary clinic. "What's this I hear about you threatening to kill Ned Copeland?" he asked.

"It's not a threat. I'm glad he's taking me seriously."

"I'm not so sure he is. One of my deputies heard him joking about it last night at the Shamrock. You're not serious, are you, Walt?"

"I'm dead serious. One way or the other that guy is going to pay for what he did."

"Killing him would be a pretty stiff punishment, don't you think?"

"Not for the suffering he caused. But I gave him a choice. I'm willing to let the court decide his punishment."

"The court can't do that if he isn't prosecuted."

"Then I'll be the one to punish him."

The sheriff shook his head in disbelief. "You're the last person I'd expect to hear talking like that. What's gotten into you?"

"Copeland went too far this time, way too far. He can't be allowed to get away with it."

"Then make him pay some other way. Hire

somebody to bust his kneecap or smash that Cadillac he takes such pride in. But don't kill him."

"The cycle would just start all over again. You saw what he's capable of doing. Next time his vengeance could be directed at my daughter or one of my grandchildren. I'm not prepared to play that kind of game."

"But you are prepared to throw your own life away just to see him punished? That doesn't make sense."

"I can forgive and forget a lot of things, Doug, but not the suffering Copeland caused. It was a vile act that simply can't go unpunished. I couldn't live with myself if it did."

Courtright started to reply, then seemed to change his mind. For a moment he stared at the wall calendar near Dr. Hux's desk, a flock of Canada geese flapping across a cold November sky. "Give me two weeks," he said, glancing at the veterinarian, then back at the calendar. "Actually I might need a little longer. Give me until November twenty-third."

"For what?"

"Bringing Copeland to justice."

"And just how do you plan to do that?"

"I've got something in mind. But it'll take until the Sunday before Thanksgiving to see if I can pull it off. You'll give me that long, won't you, Walt?"

"I gave Copeland a week," Dr. Hux said, glancing at the calendar. "I suppose another few days won't matter much in the scheme of things. But if he isn't locked up by the twenty-third ..."

"Then do whatever you have to do. But keep in mind I'll have to arrest you ... assuming Copeland doesn't kill you first."

The next morning Walter Hux bought a .38 caliber pistol and two boxes of cartridges at a gun shop in Roanoke Falls. That afternoon he started taking target practice down at the river, firing at stumps and tree trunks along the bank and rocks out in the water. Although he hoped the sheriff would find some way to put Ned Copeland behind bars, he doubted it would ever happen. He didn't really think the sheriff had a plan, figuring he was simply stalling for time. *He'll put me off as long as he can, hoping I'll finally back down. Well, it's not going to happen.*

The days passed quickly, each seeming to blend with the next. Dr. Hux spent much of his free time taking target practice. Since his mind was made up, there was no agonizing over whether he had made the right decision. The only thing left to do was wait for the deadline Courtright had set. In the meantime he would get his veterinary practice as caught up as possible and become as proficient as he could at using the pistol.

Near the end of the second week, his daughter called and invited him to spend the weekend at her farm, telling him she wouldn't be able to have him on Thanksgiving this year because she and her husband had won an all-expense-paid trip to Detroit plus tickets to see the Lions game.

"Thanksgiving in Detroit!" Dr. Hux said. "When did you and Gary ever give a hoot about football?"

"We rarely go anywhere, Dad. This trip is exactly what we need. It's completely paid for and our neighbors have agreed to take care of the farm while we're gone."

In the end he accepted her invitation. Actually he was glad it had worked out this way, knowing that if everything went as expected, he wouldn't be spending this or any other Thanksgiving with Brenda.

Thursday he called Paul Suiter, the young Roanoke Falls vet with whom he had an agreement that each would take care of the other's practice in case of an emergency. He asked if Paul considered their arrangement to cover a situation that left one of them incapacitated for a lengthy period of time, possibly permanently.

"Of course. I'd look after your practice until somebody could take it over full time. I hope you'd do the same for me. You're not having health problems, are you, Walt?"

"No, but at my age you never know what might happen."

He didn't see or talk to Doug Courtright at all that week, but Friday morning, two days before the deadline set by the sheriff, he did catch a glimpse of Ned Copeland. As they passed each other on Washington Avenue near the post office, Copeland tooted the horn of his Cadillac. Then, momentarily taking both hands from the steering wheel, he pointed with his right index finger toward his left wrist. Dr. Hux couldn't tell if the bastard was wearing a watch or not, but he was definitely sporting a smug grin.

It was twilight when Dr. Hux got back to Chockoyotte from his daughter's farm. He stopped at the clinic to check on the animals, finding then all well provided for, their cages clean and their food and water in abundant supply. He had a good crew at the clinic, and he regretted that he probably would never work with them again. Since they all knew about the puppy, he felt sure they would understand.

At home he checked his answering machine in case Doug Courtright had tried to contact him. There were no messages. To be on the safe side he called the sheriff's office, identified himself to the deputy who answered the phone, and asked if Ned Copeland had been arrested.

"No, sir," the deputy said. "Why would we arrest him?"

"That's all I need to know," Dr. Hux said and hung up. He went to the closet where he kept his pistol, inserted bullets into the chamber, and headed for his car.

A light rain had begun to fall, a raw evening with limited visibility. As he drove, the veterinarian thought about his wife, knowing she would be appalled at what he was planning to do. "Same old Walt," he imagined her saying. "When will you learn to cut folks some slack and focus on things you can actually do something about?"

"There's a difference between folks and monsters," he replied. "There comes a time when monsters have to pay."

"You'll be the one who pays. Give it up for Brenda's sake if not for yours."

"She's a big girl now, Martha. She'll get along fine regardless of what I do."

His wife didn't say any more, and Dr. Hux thought

that this time he had bested her, a rare occurrence since she was such a wise, level-headed person. He felt a sense of accomplishment until struck by the full realization of what he'd been doing, something he had done on a regular basis for the past five years: talking to and for a woman who was no longer alive.

"Maybe Copeland's right," he muttered. "Maybe I am crazy as a loon."

He thought about his daughter, wishing there had been more opportunity the past few days for them to talk. But there was nothing he could have told her, no way he could have prepared her for what he was planning to do. She wouldn't have understood anyway, he decided, any more than Doug Courtright had. A really first-rate sheriff wouldn't have tolerated what Copeland did. He'd have found a way to make the bastard pay.

"You just don't understand," Dr. Hux muttered in frustration, his words directed at his wife, the sheriff, his daughter. "This is a wrong of such magnitude it has to be redressed. If the law won't do it, then somebody has to, even if it means paying the price." The price, he knew, would be his own life or prison, depending on whether his aim was good and he was able to get off the first shot.

It was dusk as he approached Ned Copeland's house. When he realized the lights were off and the Cadillac was gone, he felt both relief and disappointment, the two conflicting emotions leaving him in a quandary as to what to do next. Pulling into the empty driveway, he decided to wait. Better get it over with tonight, he told himself. Tomorrow I might not have the nerve.

As he waited, Dr. Hux thought of his grandchildren. Being cut off from them would be the worst punishment. He'd miss them sorely. Of course he'd miss the animals too, the creatures that had been a source of enrichment his entire adult life. They had, in fact, been the one thing since his wife's death that had made him feel connected with whatever divine or positive force might exist in the universe.

"What about the critters?" he heard Martha ask. "You'll be abandoning them, you know."

"I've made arrangements for them to be taken care of until another vet can take over." He wasn't altogether pleased with his reply, but it would have to do.

As the evening wore on, Dr. Hux twice got out and walked around his car, trying to stay warm and keep from getting stiff. He considered starting the motor so he could use the heater but quickly rejected the idea. The last thing he wanted was for Ned Copeland to return home and find him dead of carbon monoxide poisoning.

During his wait he had seen the lights of only one vehicle, and that one had turned into the Judson's farm on the other side of the gut. Around nine-thirty, lights from a second vehicle appeared, and this one crossed the gut bridge and kept coming, slowing as it approached Copeland's house. Dr. Hux was surprised at how calmly he watched the car pull into the driveway. It'll be over soon, he thought with only a modicum of anxiety. Headlights curtailing his vision, he lifted the pistol from the seat, opened the door, and got out.

As he started to take aim, he realized that the car was neither white nor a Cadillac. It was a black Ford and it had a flasher on top. Quickly he lowered the pistol, trying to hide it behind his right leg.

"Better put that thing away before you hurt yourself," a familiar voice called.

"Doug? What're you doing out here?"

"Looking for you. If you really want to put more holes in Ned Copeland, you'll find him at the county hospital."

"More holes? What are you talking about?"

"He's recuperating from a deer slug in the butt. Somebody tried to make a trophy out of him. Get in and I'll tell you all about it."

After Dr. Hux got in the police cruiser, Courtright explained that yesterday was the opening day of deer season and that Ned Copeland had gone hunting as usual, only to end up getting shot himself. "They must have had a score to settle because they also shot up Ned's car. There's so many holes in it, I doubt it's going to live."

"Who did it?"

"Beats the hell out of me. Nobody saw a thing, including Ned."

Something about the way the sheriff spoke reminded the veterinarian of a little boy describing in anonymous terms a prank he had successfully pulled off. "You did it, didn't you, Doug?"

"What makes you think that?"

"The way you're talking. You can't lie worth a damn."

"Well, if I hadn't, you would have … or more likely

got yourself killed trying."

"But you didn't kill him. Apparently he'll recover."

"I didn't intend to kill him. But he'll be laid up a while. And he won't ever drive that Cadillac again. That will hurt him a lot worse than any bullet wound. Ned loved that car and he'll never be able to replace it. Hell, after all his medical bills he probably won't be able to afford a bicycle."

For the first time in what seemed like years Dr. Hux felt like laughing. The noise started low in his throat, sounding at first like a cough or an angry squirrel chattering, but it soon grew louder and more natural. When Courtright joined in, the car fairly rocked with laughter.

"How about handing over that pistol. You won't be needing it anymore, will you, Walt?"

"I might when Copeland gets out of the hospital. He'll think I was responsible."

"I've already discussed that with him. I told him you were the first person I suspected so I checked into your whereabouts and found there's about fifty people who place you in the Norlina area at the time of the shooting. I also explained there are a lot of folks around here who think he's responsible for what happened to that puppy. Any one of 'em could've shot him. I think he'll leave you alone."

Dr. Hux recalled the extraordinary amount of activity at his daughter's farm, all the people who had been in contact with him during his visit.

"You even got Brenda involved, didn't you?"

"I didn't want Copeland to have any reason whatsoever to think it was you. There was also the possibility I could've killed him. If that happened I wanted you to have an airtight alibi."

"How did you manage to get close enough to wound him without him seeing you?"

"You forget I was a darn good hunter at one time, Walt ... back before you shamed me into giving up the sport. A lot of folks used to say I was the best shot in the county." Courtright grinned. "Turns out I still am."

RAILROAD MAN (1971-2000)

At exactly six-thirty on a cold November morning in 1971, Merle Haverling made three sweeping arcs with his lantern, waited for the engineer's response—two air horn toots and a rapid clattering of bell—then climbed aboard the caboose of train # 85 for his and the train's final run from Portsmouth to Raleigh. As usual Molly Cavenaugh was uppermost in his mind.

"There's a gal over by the fence trying to get your attention," Charlie Craddock, the train's conductor, said as the caboose gave a lurch and began rolling forward. "Wouldn't be me she's waving at."

Realizing it was Molly, Merle jumped to the ground and sprinted to the fence. "What're you doing out here at this ungodly hour?"

"I'm addicted to you, Merle. You're worse than cigarettes. I wanted to see you one last time."

The horn sounded again, a long blast followed by two shorts.

"Step on it, boy!" Charlie yelled, barely competing with the sound of the engine's revving motor. "You'll get left behind."

Merle touched Molly's fingers where they gripped the fence, then bent down and kissed them. "This isn't goodbye," he said. "We'll find a way." Then he stood up, mouthed the words "I love you," and hurried after the caboose. Out of breath when he got there, he reached for the grab iron and hauled himself up onto the rear platform. When he glanced back at the receding freight yard, he was too far away to tell if Molly was still there or not.

Merle had known for months about the impending demise of the branch line from Portsmouth to Norlina, where it connected with the Seaboard System's main line. Much of the branch line had been redundant ever since the Seaboard and the Atlantic Coast Line merged, and with competition for freight increasingly fierce, the railroad had no choice but to retrench, which meant selling off unprofitable trackage when possible and abandoning the rest. So when management announced that the tracks between Norlina and Roanoke Falls would be abandoned, the news came as no surprise. What Merle wasn't prepared for was saying a final goodbye to Molly.

The previous night she had come to his room at the boarding house, and they had made love, clinging to each other long after their bodies were spent. After walking her home to the small house on Front Street where Molly and her young son lived with her mother, Merle had told her not to be surprised if someday he asked her to marry him.

"I think we'd make a great couple," she said. "But I know you've got obligations, Merle. Whatever you decide, I'll accept. Just don't leave me hanging."

"No way," he said. And at the time he had meant it.

As train # 85 rumbled through Chockoyotte, Merle pointed at a church steeple in the distance, telling Charlie that the house where he had grown up and where his parents still lived was a block south of there. A few minutes later they were in Roanoke Falls setting out flatcars stacked with pulpwood and picking up empties. Merle's first railroad job had been in that switchyard, he told Charlie. He'd hired on right after high school and had worked for the Seaboard ever since.

"Plan to make a career of it, do you?" the old conductor asked.

"Can't imagine doing anything else. Railroading's been in my blood ever since my dad took me to the depot to watch the Tidewater come in."

"I was a conductor on that train the last few years it ran. Number 18 going down and 17 coming back. Made for a long day, Merle. You aiming to be an engineer?"

"That's my goal. I was accepted in the training program a few weeks ago."

"Congratulations. I couldn't help but notice your girlfriend back there in Portsmouth. Good thing you're not married. Being a brakeman can be hell on a family. You're on call at all hours, and you spend more time on the road than you do at home. Unless you can satisfy more than one wife, you better limit yourself to being married to the railroad. Guess I'm not telling you something you don't already know."

"Not really." Merle decided not to tell Charlie he was already married, had been for almost four years. The old conductor would probably ask about his family, and he didn't feel like talking about a wife who had gotten pregnant their senior year in high school, precipitating a marriage that never would have happened otherwise.

Merle didn't notice his wife's aging Corvair in the apartment complex's parking lot, so he wasn't surprised to find their apartment empty, no sign of Betsy or their son Toby. He had just finished unpacking his suitcase when the telephone rang.

"It's me. I'm at Rex Hospital. I was going for groceries when a U-Haul truck ran a red light and slammed into my car. I've got a broken arm but otherwise I seem to be OK. Toby was out cold for a while, which scared the hell out of me, but he's conscious now. The doctor is running some tests to make sure he's all right."

"What kind of tests?" Merle said, his stomach knotting with dread.

"A brain scan and something else, I forget what it's called."

"Wasn't he strapped in his booster seat?"

"He was, but those things aren't much protection in an accident. There wasn't a thing I could've done about this, Merle. My light was green and had been for a few seconds and that damn truck came out of nowhere."

That afternoon when Merle and Betsy were finally allowed to see Toby, the boy seemed listless and withdrawn. The few words he attempted were garbled and slurred, and then he drifted off to sleep. Later a neurologist told the Haverlings that Toby apparently had suffered a Diffuse Axial Injury, a kind of trauma that can happen in a car accident when the unmoored brain lags behind the movement of the skull, thereby causing extensive tearing of nerve tissue. The brain damage that results can be either temporary or permanent.

"It's generally a good sign when a person regains consciousness so quickly after an accident, so right now I'm cautiously optimistic," the neurologist said. "But it's too early to tell how Toby will be affected in the long run. We'll know more about that in a few weeks when we'll do some follow-up tests and a more sophisticated brain scan. In the meantime I'd like Toby to remain in the hospital where he can get therapy and be monitored for any changes in his condition."

During the next few weeks, Toby's physical condition improved, but his cognitive abilities continued to deteriorate. He lost the ability to form words, the sounds he now made consisting mainly of grunts, groans, and an occasional shriek. Rarely making eye contact, he seemed lost in his own little world where he seemed neither happy nor unhappy. He once again needed to wear Pampers.

Already discouraged by Toby's regression, the Haverlings were devastated when the neurologist finally gave them a more definitive diagnosis. "I'm very sorry to have to tell you this," he said in a somber voice. "I'm afraid Toby has not only suffered damage to both sides of his brain but that damage is most likely irreversible." The doctor went on to explain that the follow-up tests he had ordered all indicated a rather bleak future for Toby. Even with therapy the boy probably would never achieve more than a limited ability to communicate, follow instructions, and perform simple tasks. Most likely he would require lifelong care and supervision.

"So what you're telling us," Merle said with tears in his eyes, "is that our son is severely retarded and always will be."

The neurologist shook his head. "I know it's of no consolation to you folks, but Toby isn't retarded. Up until the time of his accident his brain had been developing normally."

Merle and Betsy spent much of the next day talking to the hospital's social worker about how they might cope with the changes that would be taking place in their lives. The social worker explained that after Toby went home in a week or two, he would continue to receive therapy as an outpatient. When he reached the age of five, the county would begin providing schooling for him just as it does for normal children. In Toby's case it would be a special education program designed to fit his needs.

"That's the good news," she said. "The bad news is the county doesn't offer a pre-school program for disabled kids, which means your lives are going to be especially difficult this next year or so, if for no other reason than you won't be able to get a break from your son by sending him to school. No matter how much you love Toby, there will be times when you'll want to tear your hair out ... and maybe even his."

The social worker went on to say that parents with severely brain damaged children like Toby generally end up following one of two paths. They will stick with the child until he reaches an age, normally in his late teens, when it's clear that he's ready to go into a group home. Or they will be his primary caregiver for the rest of his life or theirs.

"I don't place a value judgment on either of these approaches," the woman said. "Depending on the circumstances, either one may be appropriate. Which path you choose will probably be determined by how much progress, if any, Toby makes and how difficult it is to function as his primary caregiver."

The social worker readily admitted she had little to offer the Haverlings but her sympathy. "There is one bit of advice, though, that I do have for you. County Social Services does offer Respite Care, a program I suggest you sign up for. Once you're approved, you can periodically get someone well versed in the needs of disabled children like Toby to take him off your hands for a day or two. This program must be used sparingly and is definitely not a panacea, but it's a lot better than nothing."

That night as the Haverlings sat in near silence on their living room sofa, Merle promised Betsy that he would do whatever he could to help out with Toby. "At least there won't be any more Portsmouth runs," he said. "And I'll try to avoid anything that'll keep me gone overnight."

"I was beginning to wonder if you had a girlfriend in

Portsmouth, Merle. You don't, do you?"

"No," he said with little hesitation, his feelings for Molly Cavenaugh overshadowed by his son's terrible tragedy.

Merle had met Molly on his first Portsmouth layover, having drawn the assignment most Seaboard workers dreaded, brakeman on a Saturday run. The return freight didn't leave until Monday, so he was stuck in Portsmouth for a day and a half with nothing to do.

He got a room at a boarding house used by railroad workers, and after breakfast Sunday morning, he went for a walk to check out the town. Shortly before eleven he happened on a church with a marquee out front that said "Everyone, regardless of persuasion, is welcome." Although Merle wasn't much of a church goer, he decided now might be as good a time as any to touch base with the Almighty.

Noticing that the last pew was empty except for a blonde-haired woman and a towheaded boy, Merle sat down near them. When it came time for the sermon, the minister told the congregation he planned to talk about breaking down barriers, but before getting started he wanted everyone to turn to his neighbor, introduce himself, and give that person a hug or a handshake, whichever seemed appropriate. Turning toward the woman, Merle saw that she was better looking than he originally thought. She gave him an awkward smile and slid over next to him.

"I'm Molly Cavenaugh. You're new here, aren't you?"

"Merle Haverling. I work for the Seaboard and I'm on a layover."

"I hope you don't mind hugging a total stranger."

"Not when she's as pretty as you," Merle replied, surprised by his brazenness. When they hugged, he felt something stir inside him, and when they finally separated, he had trouble focusing on the sermon.

After the service Molly introduced him to her son, a freckle-faced boy with his mother's green eyes. Tommy seemed impressed by the fact that Merle was a railroad man. "I'm going to be an engineer when I grow up," he said.

"Me too," Merle replied, and after a brief pause all three of them laughed.

Molly asked if Merle had plans for lunch, and when he said no, she invited him to eat with them. "We live with my mother. In case you're wondering, Tommy's father and I divorced a year ago."

"I'm married," Merle told her. "Does that make a difference?"

Molly took a moment to respond. "Do you happen to like fried chicken?"

"I do."

"Well, there's a restaurant close by that serves really good fried chicken. I know because my mom is a waitress there. I'll be glad to drop you off."

Merle's heart sank. "Actually, I'm not hungry right now," he said and turned to the boy. "Nice meeting you, Tommy." He started walking toward the road.

"Get your butt back here, Merle Haverling," Molly called after him. "I was just teasing you. Married or not, you deserve a decent Sunday dinner. Mom's fried chicken is better than what you'd get at any restaurant around here."

Three weeks after Toby went home from the hospital, Merle received a letter from Molly. Addressed to him in care of the Seaboard System's Raleigh subdivision, it was in his mailbox at the yardmaster's office when he returned from a freight run to Hamlet. He waited until he got to the parking lot and climbed into his pickup truck before opening it.

Dear Merle,
　I finished my classes at the career center and am now a phlebotomist at a medical group. What I do there is still considered on-the-job training, but I'm making good money for a newbie. Apparently I have a talent for drawing blood. At least my supervisor says so and none of my patients have complained. Each one fills out a questionnaire after I vampire them (ha ha), and they've all given me high marks.
　I really miss you, Merle. I hope the fact that I haven't heard from you doesn't mean you've decided to call it quits. Write when you can. Better yet, give me a call. Tommy says to tell his favorite railroad man hi and that he misses you too. We're still living with Mom and probably will be for quite a while (I'm not making <u>that</u> much money).
　　　　　　　　　　Love,
　　　　　　　　　　Molly

Gazing through the windshield at the switchyard where a shifter was making up tomorrow's freight train for Richmond, Merle thought longingly of his time with Molly. The two of them had meshed so well it soon had seemed to him that they were, in fact, already married. With Tommy accompanying them much of the time, they had taken long walks, gone out to eat, attended church, and explored the surrounding area, including parts of Norfolk and Virginia Beach. The first time they made love, it was all Merle could do to keep from crying out with joy. Afterwards, as they lay on his bed in the boarding house, he felt an almost equally intense feeling of sadness.

"What's the matter?" she asked. "Are you disappointed with me?"

"Yeah. I'm disappointed we aren't married to each other."

After church Merle usually took Tommy to the Portsmouth freight yard to watch its shifter shuttle cars from one location to another. Once when the small engine was idle, he unlocked his train's caboose and showed the boy its interior. After that, Tommy wasn't sure whether he wanted to be an engineer or a brakeman.

"Maybe I'll be a brakeman first," he said. "Just like you, Merle."

Molly's mother didn't take to Merle the way Tommy did. Though civil enough, she made no secret of her displeasure that Merle already had a family. "As long as you're married, nothing good can come of this," she told him. "I hope you realize it."

When Merle didn't reply, she asked what he planned to do about the situation.

"I don't know," he said. "I really don't know."

"Then I suggest you give it some serious thought. You're playing with my daughter's life, Merle. Tommy's too. That boy thinks you hung the moon."

A week after receiving Molly's letter, Merle wrote the letter of response that he had been dreading:

Dear Molly,

I'm sorry I waited so long to contact you but the day I got back from Portsmouth my wife and son were in a car wreck. Betsy wasn't hurt bad but Toby was. He has severe brain damage that's probably irreversible.

Molly, I never thought I'd say this but I think we should stop seeing each other. Toby is quite a handful now and needs help doing the simplest things. With him in that condition, it wouldn't be right for me to leave Betsy. And I can't fulfill my responsibilities to her or Toby if I'm a cheating husband.

Please forgive me for telling you all this in a letter. I wanted to do it in person but there's no way I can get to Portsmouth and back without Betsy realizing I've been seeing someone. She already suspects something because of my many layovers.

Tell Tommy he's a great kid and I'll really miss him. He'll make a fine railroad man or anything else he decides to be.

Molly, I can't even begin to describe how much I'll miss you. I wish we'd met a long, long time ago.

Sincerely,
Merle

The next morning he decided the letter was a coward's way out and tore it up. That evening, after returning from a freight run to Richmond, he stopped at a phone booth and called Molly, telling her pretty much what he had said in the letter. Though obviously saddened, she accepted his decision without argument. He started to tell her that if there ever came a time when Toby could pretty much take care of himself, maybe the two of them could pick up where they left off. But he knew that wouldn't be fair to Molly, so he simply told her goodbye.

It didn't take the Haverlings long to realize how hard it is to be the sole caregivers of a severely brain-damaged child. Shortly after returning home, Toby began spending most of his waking hours going from room to room looking for something to shake, spin, chew, or otherwise play with in an inappropriate fashion. If the object happened to be breakable, it often ended up broken. Several times a day he would open the refrigerator door and grab whatever struck his fancy—milk, orange juice, a pie, a bowl of Jello, a leftover from a previous meal. He would eat or drink what he wanted and dump the rest on the floor. One of his favorite activities was reaching into his pamper for a gob of feces and smearing it on himself, the floor, and the wall.

Toby's sleeping habits also changed for the worse, making it next to impossible for Merle and Betsy to get as much sleep as they needed. During the night he would spend lengthy stretches jumping up and down in his crib, rattling the slats and making loud noises which resembled the shrieks of a seagull. When their neighbors in the adjoining apartment complained, Merle said he would move Toby's crib as far from their wall as possible but that he couldn't control the noise the boy made because his brain had been damaged in a recent car accident. Although the neighbors seemed sympathetic, Betsy feared that sooner or later, a letter would appear in their mailbox threatening eviction if something wasn't done about their son's noises.

As promised, Merle did what he could to lighten Betsy's load. He dropped out of the training classes for prospective engineers and no longer put his name in for assignments requiring a layover. Periodically he was still called for such a run, but before agreeing to the assignment, he made sure respite care was available for the night in question. On the rare occasions it wasn't, he told the dispatcher that his back had gone out on him, something it periodically did, and that he would need at least one more visit to the chiropractor before he could do any of the lifting normally required of a brakeman.

A few weeks after Toby's fifth birthday, a small yellow bus with "Wake County Schools" printed on the side picked him up for the first time. Betsy was afraid he might not tolerate the twenty-minute drive to where his special education classes were held, but at the end of his first day, and whenever she inquired thereafter, the driver told her that as long as the bus remained in motion, Toby seemed completely content.

Having a break from the boy for six hours a day, five days a week did wonders for Betsy, and she seemed to blossom in front of Merle's eyes. She got a part-time job in the deli at the Food Lion and joined a weight-watcher's group. Soon she took up jogging. Though Merle saw less of her now because of her new interests and activities, he enjoyed being with her more than he ever had. She seemed less dependent on him, more of a person in her own right. Even making love to her was more pleasurable.

Merle's longing for Molly Cavenaugh did not diminish, however, and he thought of her often. He had to keep reminding himself that Betsy, after all, was his wife and the mother of his son, and if there was a reasonable chance the three of them could make a go of it, he was duty-bound to try.

Since Toby seemed to enjoy his bus rides so much, every weekend Merle and Betsy took him for a ride in the country. Before returning to their apartment, they stopped at a McDonald's or a Burger King and bought the boy a chocolate milkshake, his favorite drink.

Not long after Betsy got a job at the Food Lion, Merle resumed his training classes. For the next six months or so, things seemed to go reasonably well for him and Betsy. Then one evening a few minutes before the start of Merle's night class, the dispatcher announced that the instructor's wife had gone into premature labor and he'd taken her to the hospital. The class was postponed until the following week.

Weary from the day's freight run, Merle was glad for the night off. When he pulled up in front of his apartment, he noticed through a gap in the curtains that someone besides Betsy was in the living room, a man he'd never seen before. A moment later Betsy appeared and they began to kiss. After staring for a while in stunned silence, Merle picked up the biggest rock he could find and hurled it through the window. Then he got back in his truck and drove to the nearest bar.

When he returned to the apartment two hours later, Betsy was waiting on the sofa.

"How long have you been cheating on me?" he asked, his words slurred.

"I'm sorry, Merle. I ..."

"Answer the question, damnit! How long have you been seeing that guy?"

"Since a few weeks after I started work at the Food Lion. Bob is the manager. I was going to tell you but I couldn't find the nerve."

"Are you in love with him?"

Slowly she nodded, then took a deep breath, gathering herself for what she was about to say. "We want to get married."

Merle almost laughed. "I wish to hell I'd known about this earlier. Now it's probably too late."

"Too late for what?"

Ignoring the question, Merle went in the kitchen and used the wall phone to call the dispatcher's office. He told the woman who answered that he needed a couple days off to resolve a serious family problem. Then he stuffed a few items in his suitcase and, without saying another word to Betsy, got in his truck. Three and a half hours later he checked into a cheap motel near the Portsmouth freight yard. Although bone weary, he was too wrought up to fall asleep until shortly before dawn.

The sun was halfway up the eastern sky when Merle

woke up. At first he didn't know where he was, but reality quickly set in, accompanied by a wave of anxiety that Molly Cavenaugh might no longer be available. He took a quick shower, then sat for a while on the edge of the bed trying to collect himself before making the call.

The familiar voice of Molly's mother came on the line, a good sign, Merle thought, until she told him Molly no longer lived there. When he asked for her new phone number, the woman told him Molly was married.

Merle was devastated. The worst case scenario, he had thought, was that she wouldn't want anything more to do with him because so much time had elapsed or because she had found someone else. Either way, he figured, he would still have a chance.

"When?" he asked, barely above a whisper.

"A little over a month ago."

"Where does she live?"

"Richmond. Don't try to contact her. She married a nice man. Ray will make a good father for Tommy."

"What's Ray's last name?"

"That's none of your business. You're out of the picture now, Merle. Leave my daughter alone."

By the time Merle got back to his apartment, Betsy and Toby were gone and so were most of their belongings. Merle wasn't surprised, wasn't even particularly angry. He didn't blame Betsy for what she had done, knowing he had played a similar game himself. She just turned out to be better at it than he was. When the music stopped, she wasn't the one left without a chair.

That night Merle got drunk at a bar where railroad workers hung out. He didn't mention Betsy, explaining his presence by saying he'd been working long hours and needed a night out. He slept most of the next day and probably would have gotten drunk again had the dispatcher not called to see if things had simmered down enough for Merle to make a freight run to Hamlet.

"Pencil me in," he replied. "And put my name back in the pool for anything that comes along. I'm a free man now."

After hanging up the phone, he broke into sobs.

Merle had been divorced for over two years when he was finally promoted to engineer. In the meantime he had moved to a smaller apartment, though it was in a better neighborhood than where he and Betsy had lived. She had agreed to joint custody of Toby, and Merle continued seeing the boy on a regular basis. As he and Betsy once did, he often took Toby for long rides in the country. Not having her to hold the boy's milkshakes proved problematic until Merle decided to let Toby try one while in McDonald's parking lot. The boy hardly spilled a drop.

Though he doubted Toby understood, or even cared, what was being said, Merle always talked to him during their rides. He pointed out by name many of the objects they passed—cows, horses, silos, hay rolls, tractors, the various crops in the fields, different types of trees, an occasional pond or lake. He also asked Toby a lot of questions. Was his stepfather treating him well? Was he getting plenty to eat? Did he like his special ed classes? Was he learning a lot? Merle didn't expect replies. He merely hoped Toby would interpret the questions as a show of interest, Merle's way of saying "I still care about you, son. I haven't completely forsaken you."

He told Toby about some of the things happening in his own life. He described the diesel engines he operated and some of the runs he made. When Merle's back started giving him trouble, he told Toby about that. "The worst thing I can do is sit for long periods of time," he said. "It's not so bad in a C-420 Alco or an SDP-35 because their cabs are big enough to stand up in and even walk around a bit. But those geeps can be a real pain in the butt ... and back."

If Merle's back happened to be bothering him more than usual, he would take Toby to Raleigh's Oakwood cemetery where he could keep his truck—a newer one now—moving enough to satisfy the boy. If his back stiffened or started aching, he would pull over, get out, and do some stretching exercises. As long as his limbering up didn't take too long, Toby didn't seem to mind.

One day while driving through the cemetery, Merle told the boy about Molly. "I hired a private detective to find out her last name," he said. "It's Fesperman. I knew she lived in Richmond and her husband's first name was Ray, so the next time I was in Richmond on a layover, I checked the phone book and sure enough there was a Raymond R. Fesperman. I called the number and after a couple rings Molly answered. I wanted to find out if she was happy. Not that she'd give me an honest answer. But if she didn't, I figured I could tell from her voice how things were. Just as I was about to identify myself, I realized I had no right trying to insinuate myself back into her life, no right at all. I'd had my chance and let it slip away ... with a little help from you and your mom, of course. I don't mean it was your fault or hers. It wasn't anybody's fault. Your mother and I just weren't a good fit, Toby, not like Molly and me anyway. At least that's what I've always believed. I'll never know for sure because I hung up without saying a word. I made up my mind to forget all about Molly Cavenaugh. But do you know something? I don't think I'll ever be able to do that. She'll probably haunt me until the day I die."

Eventually a ruptured disk cut short Merle's career as an engineer. By then the Seaboard System and the Chessie System had merged, forming CSX. Since the company needed people with Merle's experience, it offered him a job at its Richmond headquarters recruiting future employees and teaching classes to prospective conductors and engineers as well as to new hires. He was reluctant to accept such a job because of Toby, who at the age of nineteen had moved into a group home in Raleigh. But since Merle wasn't ready for retirement and didn't have anything else in mind, he took the job, discovering that he liked the work even better than he had being an engineer. Almost every weekend he would drive back to Raleigh and spend a few hours with Toby at his group home.

Whenever he talked to potential hires about opportunities with CSX, Merle always made sure they understood the importance of having a strong back, especially for anyone starting out as a brakeman or aspiring to be an engineer. And he always warned them, as Charlie Craddock had warned him, about the dangers of getting married until at least a few years after hiring on. Sometimes he even found himself quoting Charlie: "Unless you can satisfy more than one wife, you better limit yourself to being married to the railroad."

During the spring following the Y2K scare, Richmond's Mills E. Godwin High School asked CSX to provide a representative for its Career Day. The railroad sent Merle. As he was giving his usual spiel to a group of students, he noticed a blonde girl in the second row who looked so familiar he had to take several deep breaths before continuing his talk.

Merle spoke for another forty minutes or so and then opened the session to questions. The first one he got was from a boy who asked whether he was married.

"I was once ... back in the day."

"How old were you when you tied the knot, Mr. Haverling?"

"Not much older than you folks. I got married the summer I finished high school."

"How long did the marriage last?" another student asked, and there was muted laughter.

"Six years. It wasn't the railroad's fault. We would have probably split up anyway."

"How come you never married again?" the blonde girl in the second row asked.

"Never found the right person," Merle replied after a moment, working hard to maintain his composure.

"Now if you folks don't mind, I'd like to focus on your futures instead of my past. Please keep your questions pertinent to the reason I'm here, which is to tell you about the railroad industry and the kind of job opportunities you can expect over the next few years."

Finally when there were no more questions and the students were leaving the room, Merle asked the blonde girl to wait a minute, that he had a question he wanted to ask her.

"Sure. What is it, Mr. Haverling?"

"You remind me a lot of someone I used to know. I'm wondering if you might be related."

"What's this person's name?"

"Molly. Molly Cavenaugh. At least that was her last name back then. It's Fesperman now."

"It's still Cavenaugh," the girl said with a look of surprise. "Mom dropped the Fesperman after she and my dad divorced. I'm Jessica Fesperman. How'd you know my mom?"

"It's ... it's a long story," Merle said, not knowing what else he could or should say. "You ... uh ... you have a half-brother named Tommy, right? He must be over thirty by now."

The girl's face darkened. "He would've been. He died in a training accident in the army. He was nineteen."

A wave of sadness washed over Merle. "Tommy was just a kid when I knew him ... a really nice kid."

"He was a great brother too. You must have met him and Mom when they lived in Portsmouth."

"I did. I met them while I was on a layover there. Your mother and I went out together a few times. Does she still live in Richmond?"

"No, after she and my dad split up, she moved back to Portsmouth to be near my grandmother." The girl glanced at her watch. "I'm sorry to have to cut this short, Mr. Haverling, but I've got an appointment soon and I need to get some lunch first."

A few minutes later Merle was back in his truck, which was still in the school's parking lot. Using his cell phone he called his office secretary.

"Ginny, it's Merle. I need you to do me a favor. Call directory assistance and see if you can get a phone number for Molly Cavenaugh in Portsmouth. If you can't get a number for her, try Molly Fesperman. And if neither of those names shows up, try Molly's mother's name, which is Florence Booth."

Five minutes later, the secretary called him back. Molly wasn't listed but a Florence Booth was. Merle started to dial her number, then stopped. Why would Ms. Booth give out her daughter's phone number or current address to him of all people? Even if she did, Molly would be middle-aged now, a woman who had gone through two failed marriages and whose son had died before he reached twenty. Why would she want anything to do with him at this point in her life? So many years had gone by, she might not even remember him.

Merle closed the cover of his cell phone and set it on the passenger seat. Slowly he buckled his seat belt, then cranked the truck's engine to life. Taking hold of the emergency break, he hesitated for a moment before releasing it and several more seconds before putting the truck in gear and easing it toward the parking lot's exit.

His mind still focused on Molly, Merle drove slowly on his way home. He thought of the day they met and how she had teased him by pretending to withdraw her Sunday dinner invitation. He thought of the Virginia Beach amusement park where the two of them held hands as they watched a miniature passenger train circle the grounds with Tommy sitting so proudly in the seat directly behind the engineer. He thought of Molly standing on the far side of the freight yard fence, having gotten up long before dawn to be with him one last time.

Maybe there's still a chance, he told himself as he turned into his apartment complex. Maybe she hasn't found someone else yet. And if she hasn't, then maybe, just maybe, she won't mind hearing from me after all these years ...

After pulling into his designated parking spot, Merle sat for a while gazing through the windshield at nothing in particular, still unsure what to do.

"You'll never know unless you try," he said at last and reached for his cell phone.

CINDY'S POEM (2004)

When I saw Cindy's name on the folded sheet of paper that accompanied the poem, I wasn't surprised. Cindy Laughton was my best student, a feisty sort with a nose ring and spiked lavender hair who sat in the front row of my two o'clock class. She made a point of never letting a classmate—or me, for that matter—get away with what she referred to as "bullshit with a capital B." When I told her I didn't think *bullshit* was an appropriate word to use in an 11th grade English class, she said she'd henceforth call it *bovine excrement*.

She called her submission "For Christ's Sake," a title I hoped wouldn't be followed by a maudlin religious ditty. It wasn't.

> What is it with these people
> Who raise high the banner of Christianity
> While making war against the very groups

Jesus would have befriended?
To hear their angry talk you'd never know
Helping the poor and loving one's neighbor
Were the cornerstones of His teaching.
They have different agendas, these neo-Christian soldiers
Who never met a social program
They didn't try to hack to pieces.
They exalt the fetus and fight for its rights
But ignore the cries of those to misery born.
They help themselves instead of the poor
And being the chosen ones, at least in their own eyes,
They fully expect to enter the kingdom of heaven.
Didn't they read the part about the needle's eye
Or think it applied to them?

It used to be the blacks they hated
These mean-spirited zealots of the right
Who create God in their own image
And then wreak havoc in his name.
Now it's the gays they crusade against,
Making their struggle for equality a Herculean task.
What is it that keeps these intolerant crusaders
From seeing the obvious:
That people don't choose the gender of their attraction
Anymore than they do the color of their skin?
Jesus stood for inclusiveness.
He would have driven their bigoted asses

From the temple just as surely
As he did the moneychangers.

As faculty adviser to *Winged Words*, Chockoyotte High School's modest attempt at a literary magazine, I had asked my students to submit only their best work: stories, poems, and essays of substance. As I sat staring at Cindy's submission, I almost wished I'd requested fluff.

The following afternoon, at the end of my two o'clock class, I told Cindy I'd like a word with her.

"Yes, Mr. Andrews?" she said after collecting her books and approaching my desk. Her tone was softer than the one she normally used in class, which had an edge to it. She had a pretty face, her nose ring and outlandish hair notwithstanding, but she was heavier than most girls her age, especially in the hips and legs. One time in the hall I heard a football player ask when she planned to sign up for Jenny Craig, to which she replied without missing a beat: "Maybe this summer. Right now I'm too busy doing volunteer work for Jocks Without Brains."

"I'd like to talk to you about the poem you submitted to *Winged Words*," I told her. "Have you got a few minutes?"

"It's that bad, huh?"

"Actually, it's very good."

"Then why am I getting the feeling it's been rejected?"

I chuckled. "If I were grading these submissions, yours would get an A plus. Maybe you better sit down, Cindy. You won't miss your ride home or anything, will you?"

She shook her head. "Mom's sick today so I got the car." She eased into the straight-backed chair next to my desk and dumped her books on the floor. "So what's wrong with my poem?"

"Nothing. You've said something significant and you've said it very well." I paused, wishing I didn't have to say anything more. "But what you've written is more like an essay than a poem. Except for being in stanza form, it really doesn't use any poetic devices."

"You mean like meter and rhyme?"

"I don't think your poem would lend itself to rhyme, though you might try it in a few places. The meter isn't a problem either."

"So what's the problem?"

"You're saying everything straight out, like you would in an essay. I don't mean that as criticism. What you've written is exceptionally good, especially for a high school student."

She gave me an impatient look. "Why don't you cut to the chase, Mr. Andrews. Is what I submitted going to fly or not?"

"I think it will. First, though, I'd like you to read a few poems by some established poets and pay close attention to how they achieve their effects. Then I hope you'll rework your poem accordingly. If you do, I think you can get it published in a literary magazine. A real one, I mean, not just *Winged Words*."

"Really?" Her face brightened. "You think it's that good?"

"It's absolutely first rate." I opened the copy of *Writer's Market* I'd brought with me that morning to a page I'd previously marked with a notecard and handed the book to Cindy. "This section pertains to literary magazines and what they're looking for. Usually they don't pay anything, just a contributor's copy or two, but it's a real honor to be published in one of them."

She scanned a few entries. "If my poem gets published in *Winged Words* first, would these mags still be interested?"

I shook my head. "Almost all of them want previously unpublished work," I said, neglecting to add that being published in an unknown high school mag probably wouldn't disqualify her.

She flipped through more pages, read a few more entries, then handed the book back to me. "Thanks, Mr. Andrews, but I'm pretty busy right now. Maybe down the road a bit I'll learn more about what real poetry is like and try another poem."

"I wish you wouldn't give up on this one so quickly. I'll be glad to help you work on it."

"I don't have the time. My mom's having trouble making ends meet, so last week I got a part-time job at McDonald's. Isn't what I wrote good enough to be published in *Winged Words*? I mean, you did say it's first rate."

I took a deep breath and slowly let it out. "I don't think your poem is appropriate material for *Winged Words*."

Her eye brows narrowed. "Why?"

"The subject matter ... it's pretty strong stuff."

She sighed. "You want me to take out the phrase *bigoted asses*, don't you?"

"No, I think the way you ended the poem is

effective."

"Oh yeah? Then what *is* the problem?"

"I hate to say this but I think your poem would be offensive to a lot of people."

"Bullshit! Most students don't even read *Winged Words*. Those who do wouldn't have a problem with what I wrote. At least most of them wouldn't."

"Probably not. But some of their parents might, not to mention Dr. Hartung."

Disappointment mingled with anger on her face. "Why'd you tell everybody you were looking for substance if you were going to turn up your nose when you got it?" she asked on the verge of tears.

"I'm sorry, Cindy. To tell the truth, I never thought I'd get a piece of writing like yours. One that's so ... well, powerful."

"You never expected to get one that told the truth, you mean, don't you? Listen, Mr. Andrews. I worked my butt off on that poem. I did exactly what you asked us to do. I wrote something I'm familiar with and really care about, and I revised until my fingers ached. For your information, I've got a retarded brother who's in a group home. Tyrone needs some expensive dental work and with all the cuts in social programs lately there's no funding for that kind of thing." She hesitated. "I also know something about gay people because I happen to be a lesbian."

She paused again, apparently expecting a reaction of shock or disappointment or maybe a few words of condescending sympathy. What she got was a slight nod of my head as though she'd just told me she was a vegetarian.

"Now you're telling me what I wrote is excellent but not suitable for *Winged Words*," she continued. "That's worse than bullshit. That's censorship. You're not a faculty adviser, Mr. Andrews. You're a damn censor."

With that she collected her books and stormed out of the classroom.

Rogers Hartung, Chockoyotte High School's principal, isn't one of my favorite people, though when he hired me two years ago he seemed like an affable, easy-going man. It didn't take me long to realize that most of the teachers referred to him as "Doctor No-Heart-All-Tongue" for good reason. Nevertheless, I made an appointment to see him during my free period the following day.

"Come in, Bart," he said pleasantly as I stood in the doorway of his office. "What's on your mind?"

"I hate to bother you, sir," I said as I approached his desk. "This is one of the submissions for possible publication in *Winged Words*." I handed him a copy of Cindy's poem. "I'm not quite sure what to do with it."

"Have a seat and I'll take a look."

I sat down in one of the visitor's chairs facing his desk and watched him read, trying to figure out from his expression what his verdict would be. He seemed more amused than anything else, but when he looked up, he wasn't smiling.

"What makes you think this is suitable material for *Winged Words*?" he asked.

"It's head and shoulders above all the other submissions as far as the quality of writing goes. And it deals with an issue that's timely and, in my opinion at least, quite important."

He gave me a quizzical look. "You like the gays, do you, Bart?"

A chill of fear went up my spine. "I sympathize with them," I replied, not sure I'd have had the nerve to say that if I hadn't been married.

He nodded. "I think your sympathy is misplaced, but that's neither here nor there. The important thing is the student who wrote this so-called poem needs counseling. Who is he?"

The question took me by surprise. "I ... I don't know. I have a rule that submissions must be unsigned. I don't want any of the readers, myself included, to be prejudiced one way or the other by who the author happens to be."

"Not a bad idea. But how do you know who the author of a particular piece is when it comes time for publication?"

"Each submission is accompanied by a folded sheet of paper with the author's name on it."

"I see. Aren't you the least bit curious as to the identity of this particular author?"

"Yes, sir, I am. But since the student readers haven't seen the poem yet, I'd rather not know the author's identity until they have their shot at it."

Dr. Hartung seemed to reflect on what I'd just told him. Then he slowly tore the paper into small pieces. "The decision of our student readers is that this poem lacks sufficient merit for publication in *Winged Words*," he said and dropped the pieces into the wastebasket next to his desk. "You don't actually think hogwash like that is appropriate material for a high school literary magazine, do you, Bart?"

"Well, I ..."

He waved off whatever I was going to say. "What this particular student wrote isn't just wrongheaded. If it's read by impressionable minds—and it certainly would be—it could be downright dangerous. It reminds me of the nonsense masquerading as wisdom in Salinger's *Catcher in the Rye*. Have you read that novel?"

"Yes, sir." Actually I'd been planning to ask permission to teach it next year, assuming my contract is renewed.

"What do you think of it?"

"I ... I think it's a good novel."

He gave me a look of forbearance similar to the way a parent might react to the opinion of a misguided child. "Well, you're still young. Hopefully someday you'll see that book for what it is, an overrated piece of claptrap." He stood up and extended his hand. "Thanks for stopping by, Bart. It always makes sense to look before you leap. Next time, though, if it's something this cut and dried, you won't need to check with me, will you?"

"No, sir," I said, standing up and taking his hand. "I guess not."

It took me a week of soul-searching to decide what to do about Cindy's poem. During that time she missed class twice and looked uncharacteristically bored the other days. When her classmates said things she normally would have taken issue with, she didn't respond. I didn't dare call on her for fear of riling her up.

When the bell signaled the end of Friday's class, I asked her to stop by my desk. She took her time collecting her books, then sauntered over, giving me a look she might have reserved for Pat Robertson or Franklin Graham.

"What is it now?" she asked, the edge in her voice back and sharper than ever.

"I've got a favor to ask. I know you're not going to like it, but please hear me out before saying no. I want you to write another poem for *Winged Words*. The subject matter can be similar to the one you've already submitted. In fact, it can be the same, if you want. The wording will have to be different though. When Dr. Hartung reads this year's edition of *Winged Words*, I can't afford for him to think your poem was written by the same person who wrote 'For Christ's Sake.'"

Then I told her about the incident in Dr. Hartung's office.

"You actually showed *him* my poem?" She looked at me like I'd lost my mind.

"I was hoping he'd recognize what a good effort it was and give me the go-ahead to submit it to the student readers."

"Why would you need his go-ahead for that?"

"My contract runs out this spring. I didn't want to jeopardize my chances of having it renewed. If I had it to do over again, I wouldn't have involved Dr. Hartung."

"You'd have rejected my poem outright?"

"No. For starters I'd have done a better job of explaining the situation to you. Then I'd have done what I'm doing now—ask you to write another poem."

She started to walk away, then turned back around. "I already explained why I can't do that, Mr. Andrews. When you flip burgers three hours every evening, there's usually not enough time left for regular homework."

I nodded. "Tomorrow I'm going to assign your class another theme. It'll be due in three weeks. That assignment will pertain to everyone in the class but you, Cindy, assuming you agree to work on another poem. When the other students turn in their themes, you can turn in your second poem. If it's even close to being as good as your first one, I'll give it an A plus. Then I'll pass it on to the student readers of *Winged Words* for their evaluation."

"If it's got the same theme as my first one, won't you have the same problem with Dr. Hartung?"

"This time I won't ask for his advice."

"But if it gets published in *Winged Words*, he'll probably see it."

"That's why I want you to call it something other than 'For Christ's Sake.' And don't use any of the same phrases you used in your original poem. One more thing, Cindy ... and this is important. As you're working on the poem, keep in mind that a butterfly or a bumblebee can accomplish just as much as a freight train, sometimes more."

"What's that supposed to mean?"

"A poem doesn't have to steamroll the reader in order to be effective."

She nodded but still seemed skeptical. "What if my new poem is good but the student editors react the same way Dr. Hartung did to my first one?"

"I doubt that will happen. But if it does, I have a right as faculty adviser to invoke what's called a grandfather clause, which means if I think a submission is especially worthy but the staff rejects it, it gets published anyway. I've never overridden the student readers, but if necessary I will with your poem ... on one condition."

She gave me a look that said here we go again. "Which is?"

"You start participating in class again. It's been on life support ever since you clammed up."

When this year's edition of *Winged Words* came out, I gave a copy to each of my students and asked the other English teachers to distribute copies to each of theirs. At the end of my two o'clock class, Cindy came up to my desk and thanked me for everything I'd done.

"I didn't have to invoke the grandfather clause," I told her. "All but one of the student readers liked your poem."

"Carlton Flynn," she snorted, referring to a senior with an ultra-conservative bent.

"Not even Shakespeare could please everybody," I replied.

"I know. By the way, how many of the *Winged Words* staff are seniors?"

"Three. Would you like to join up next year?"

"Maybe."

"I'd love to have you on the staff, Cindy. But after Dr. Hartung reads this issue, I've got a feeling he'll decide the faculty adviser's job should go to someone else."

Her face clouded with concern. "I hope you don't catch any flack because of me. I've still got second thoughts about the title. If you'd just let me call it 'Onward Christian Soldiers,' Dr. Hartung wouldn't have a way to tie the two poems together."

"That would make it sound like an anti-Christian poem, which it isn't. The title is perfect, Cindy."

"It leaves you vulnerable."

I shrugged. "Every once in a while, you have to go up against old Ben just to keep on calling yourself a dog."

"Say what?"

"Just referring to something in a Faulkner novella you'll probably read in college."

After she left the classroom, I stared for a while at the open doorway, half expecting Rogers Hartung to appear. Finally I opened my copy of *Winged Words*, turned to a page near the end of the thin volume, and began to read.

Neo-Christian Soldiers
by
Cindy Laughton

> Across the land they march
> From sea to shining sea
> Right Right Right Right
> Carrying high their religious banner
> And a message for you and me
> Right Right Right Right

RED CLAY AND BRUNSWICK STEW

No husband, no job, and one in the oven?
Don't mess with it, let it grow
The good book is clear
You must reap what you sow
Right Right Right Right

If you're gay or a lesbian
Forget about your rights
These righteous straight shooters
Have you squarely in their sights
Right Right Right Right

Watch out you Darwinians
God's soldiers are marching through
You once made monkeys of them
Now they'll make mincemeat out of you
Right Right Right Right

Beware you empathetic doctors
You've got the most to lose
If you keep on practicing
A woman's right to choose
Right Right Right Right

You writers on their wrong side
Your goose they will cook
Watch out Judy Blume
Better censor that next book
Right Right Right Right

The list seems endless
Of evil they will fix

John W. Daniel

There's Michael Moore, Sponge Bob,
Even the Dixie Chicks
Right Right Right Right

There's Harry Potter and Jimmy Carter
To them a dangerous fool
And all those misguided souls
Who oppose prayer in the schools
Right Right Right Right

Relentlessly they march
Slashing programs for the poor
We don't need it half as much
As they do for the war
Right Right Right Right

On and on they trample
Their eyes on their ultimate goal
Confident that once they reach it
Satan himself will be under control
Right Right Right Right

There it is up ahead
The wall they intend to smash
Right Right Right Right
The thing they fear the most
And most love to hate
Right Right Right Right
That long-standing barrier
Between Church and State.

Rereading it for probably the tenth time, I still felt

chills of pride. A different kind of chill occurred when I heard the crackle of the intercom followed by the voice of Dr. Hartung's secretary summoning me to his office.

THE PRODIGAL (2005)

Alan Buchannan was leaving Greensboro's Forest Lawn Cemetery when he was approached by two young males wearing baggy jean shorts and rumpled, oversized T-shirts. The taller one, who was white, had stained, crooked teeth and a tattoo of a snake's head on his right arm, its mouth open, its fangs prominent. The other, who was black, had a lithe, muscular body and wore a baseball cap with the brim turned backwards.

"Hey, mister," the white youth called. "Bet you don't know how many dead folks are buried out here." He extended his hand in a sweeping gesture that took in the entire cemetery.

Alan stared at the boy, wondering why he had made such a statement. "I have no idea."

"All of 'em," the boy said and broke into a spasm of laughter. "Every single fuckin' one of 'em. Ha, ha, ha, ha—got ya, didn't I?"

"Some people might consider that funny," Alan replied and started to walk on. "I'm not one of them."

The black boy jumped in front of him, blocking his path. "Can't you see this a toll road, man? You don't go no further 'til you pay for the privilege."

The white boy moved closer. "In case you haven't realized it, this is a muggin'. Now hand over your wallet ... unless you want the number of dead in this skull orchard to rise by one."

"You picked the wrong victim," Alan said calmly. "You won't get a cent from me."

The black boy chuckled. "This Tom turkey got a learning disability, Snake. How 'bout givin' him a little somethin' to smarten him up."

The white youth's fist shot forward, but Alan avoided it by stepping to one side. His own fist landed squarely against the boy's face, sending him reeling backward into the grass.

"What are you, man, a boxer or somethin'?"

"I boxed some in college." Alan turned to the black boy. "You don't want to try your luck too, do you?"

A knife appeared in the boy's hand, the blade springing forward with the flick of a finger. "Maybe you'd like to try some of this."

"If I have to take that away from you, your next stop will be a hospital," Alan said. "Better put it away and save yourself some grief."

"Stick him, Dennis. Stick the cocky son of a bitch."

The black boy took a step forward, then stopped when Alan raised his fists to chest level. After a moment he closed the knife and eased it back into his pocket.

"You win, man ... for now. Next time you better bring more'n your fists."

"I've got more," Alan said, thinking of the pistol in his car's glove compartment. He had bought it after learning that Jake Smyrna was going to be paroled. Even though it was the man's third drunk driving conviction and this time he had killed two people, all the punishment he had received was two years in jail. In less than a week he would be out on the street. Sooner or later he'd be back behind the wheel ....

"Next time'll be different, man. We promise you that."

Alan walked away from the would-be muggers, putting them out of his mind as easily as if they had been a pair of gnats he'd brushed aside. It was a large cemetery and he still had a ways to go before reaching the gate. He took the same route as always, a winding tarmac path that led past an assortment of markers. The only ones he even vaguely noticed were the obelisks, which reminded him of grotesque chess pieces, pawns with crosses on top.

As he approached the wrought-iron gate, he noticed an old woman sitting under a cluster of pine trees next to a rectangular stone slab. She looked familiar and when she shifted her position, Alan recognized her. Although his first impulse was to continue on to his car, he left the path and headed toward her.

The old woman glanced up, showed no sign of recognition, and returned to her work. She was transferring flowers from a straw basket into a large urn, stripping wet newspaper from the stems before arranging the flowers. The marker beside her bore the name Alan suspected.

"Synthetic arrangements are a bit more practical," she announced before he could speak. "They require no maintenance, and I must admit they look better than that awful mess." She nodded toward a withered pile of petals, stems, and leaves at the foot of the grave.

"Many people such as myself find it impossible to get to the cemetery on a regular basis," she continued, beginning to unwrap newspaper from a final cluster of gladioli. "Yet we'd very much like to keep something pretty and alive on the graves of our loved ones. Artificial flowers just won't do. They're so ... inanimate. There's a solution to this problem, of course, and I proposed it in a still-unpublished letter to the editor of the *Daily News*. The city should provide the service of periodically watering all vases and pots and urns that contain real flowers and plants."

Same old Miss Beck, Alan reflected and couldn't help smiling at his remembrance of Miss Sue saying her sister should have been a trial lawyer because she always had a "case" to argue and invariably presented it as though everyone around her was an eager member of a jury, anxious to listen.

"A few more faucets could be installed here and there to facilitate the watering." She placed the last of the gladioli into the nearly full vase, meticulously arranging and rearranging the flowers. "Then a handful of workers, if they didn't dawdle, could perform the job nicely, it seems to me, in a couple of hours. Twice a week should be sufficient." She leaned back to better inspect her floral arrangement. "Though it would be nice if the service were provided each and every sunny day." She nudged a final snapdragon into place. "Of course, miracles couldn't be expected with cut flowers like these. But how comforting to be able to set out a pot with something rooted and growing and have confidence the sun wouldn't shrivel it beyond redemption the first hot day." She paused, timing the slow lift of her head so the meeting of the jury's eyes coincided with the request for a verdict. "What do you think of my idea, Mr. uh ..."

"I rather like it, Miss Beck."

The surprise took a moment to register. Recognition shone in her eyes, then delight animated her face. "Why, the Prodigal returneth!" She made an immediate effort to stand.

"Don't get up. Here, I'll sit down with you." Alan eased himself to the ground, which was soft, more pine straw than grass.

"I can hardly believe my eyes." The old woman extended her hand, beaming affection. "Mr. Buchannan, is it really you?"

He took her outstretched hand, gently squeezing it. "It's good to see you again, Miss Beck."

"It's good to see you, sir. But you shouldn't have let me babble on like that. If I'd known it was you, I wouldn't have made such a fool of myself."

"No sense interrupting a good idea."

"You're just humoring an old woman. You know it wouldn't work."

"I doubt the city would fund it, but I can see it as a church project, possibly an interdenominational one. Maybe if you mentioned it to Bill Duncan ..."

"That man doesn't have your imagination, Mr. Buchannan. He'd think me a fool. Anyway, I didn't really expect anything to come of it. Just another of my impracticalities, as Sue used to call them. The pleasure is in the dreaming ... and of course, the proposing."

"I'm sorry about Miss Sue," Alan said. "I didn't realize she'd died until I saw her headstone."

"She thought the world of you, Mr. Buchannan. I remember the last night of her life she spoke of you. If only things had been different, she lamented, and you were still with us. Of course, we'd both expressed that sentiment many times before. But somehow the urgent way Sue said it that night was different, as though she knew her time had come and you wouldn't be here to officiate ..."

Alan felt strange hearing his old parishioner speak of her sister's death, having always thought of Miss Beck and Miss Sue as inseparable. Even when he had visited them in their apartment, they had sat side by side in matching rockers in front of his place of honor, the prickly, high-backed monstrosity that had once been their father's favorite chair.

"Your replacement doesn't visit me like you did, Mr. Buchannan. Mr. Duncan isn't exactly what you'd call a boon to the senior citizen."

Alan smiled but said nothing. From where he sat he could see, just beyond a row of poplar trees, the twin stones that marked the graves of his wife and daughter.

"I'd be most pleased to hear about your new parish. Even though I've hardly given you a chance to get a word in edgewise, you'll find me an eager listener."

A breeze ruffled the leaves of a nearby oak tree, then

made a soughing noise in the pines overhead.

"I don't live in Chockoyotte anymore, Miss Beck," he said, hoping he could get away with a minimum of explanation. "I live in Chapel Hill now."

"Oh? You've got another parish already?"

Alan hesitated. "Actually I don't have a parish."

A look of concern spread over the old woman's face. "You don't?"

He considered telling her that he was on a leave of absence but decided he owed her the truth. "I resigned from the ministry."

The old woman's hand flew up from her lap and hovered near his arm, then tugged briefly at his sleeve. "You don't mean it, Mr. Buchannan. Why?"

"I wasn't right for the job anymore."

A wave of sadness washed over her face. "It's because of what happened to your family, isn't it?"

Alan felt like saying Death had happened to his family. Not Miss Sue's kind, which provided a gentle release after a reasonable span of years, but an unnatural, unjust, monstrous thing that snatched life from its victims like a brutal psychopath.

"Mainly that, yes," he said.

Miss Beck toyed with her handkerchief and the folds and creases of her dress, and Alan stared vaguely at the row of tenement houses beyond the hedge. He wondered if the boys who had tried to rob him lived there. It was a bad neighborhood and getting worse.

"People need ministers, Mr. Buchannan. I don't mean any fool who dons a vestment and a clerical collar and preaches a sermon and passes a wafer and the wine and utters a benediction. Mr. Duncan performs all the appropriate churchly functions with a bearing as dignified as you please, but that doesn't make him a good minister. No, sir. The ministry isn't from eight to twelve-thirty on Sundays, not especially anyway. Nor is it just marriages and funerals and baptisms and fund raising and the like. The ministry is here!" She placed a hand against her chest. "The person who makes the heart feel better, that's a minister. You did it for my sister and you did it for me. I'm sure you've done it for a lot of other people too."

"I felt different about things in those days. What I feel now ... well, a minister can't feel that way and still function."

"What is it that you feel?"

"Resentment, contempt ... even hatred. What happened to Mary Lilly and Kate made me realize I don't really love mankind. I don't even like it very much."

"That's not you, Mr. Buchannan. I know it's not you."

"It's me now, I'm afraid. It's not a big deal, Miss Beck. Things change. Life goes on."

She looked at him with a mixture of sympathy and despair. "It's a big deal to me."

"I'm sorry," Alan said. "I'm just not the same person I used to be." Then, since there was really nothing else left to say, he stood up. "I guess I better get going."

The old woman made a faltering effort to rise. "My legs have gone to sleep. Will you help me up?"

Alan took her outstretched hands and slowly pulled her to her feet.

"I'm all right now. It was good of you to stop and visit with me, Mr. Buchannan."

All the spirit had gone from her voice, making Alan wish he had made more of an effort to pretend things were different.

"Can I give you a ride home?" he asked, remembering that she had never driven a car in her life.

"No, thank you. I'd like to stay here a while longer. Then I have some shopping to do."

"I don't mind waiting. I'll take you wherever you'd like to go. This isn't a very safe neighborhood."

"The bus stops just outside the gate, so I don't have far to walk. Thank you anyway."

Every other time Alan had been with her she had practically begged him to stay longer. Now she was clearly ready for him to go. He couldn't blame her. He glanced around the cemetery to make sure the muggers weren't lurking nearby, waiting for him to leave so they could accost her.

"I'm sorry I let you down, Miss Beck. I ... I shouldn't have stopped."

When she didn't reply, he leaned over and hugged her, feeling her tears against his cheek. Finally he kissed her forehead, told her goodbye, and headed for the gate.

When he reached the parking lot, the sight of the two would-be muggers walking back across the street gave him a start. He wasn't afraid, fear being an emotion that had dried up with the deaths of his wife and daughter. The fact that the boys were heading in his direction and one was carrying a baseball bat made no difference. Alan didn't alter his pace; if they got to him before he reached his car, so be it.

The youths seemed in no particular hurry either and didn't close on him until after he was behind the wheel. A few feet from the hood, they separated, the one with the bat, the white boy, walking to the driver's side.

"The good news is you won't have to worry about this shitmobile gettin' stolen no matter where you park it."

As the bat lifted, Alan withdrew the pistol from the glove compartment and pointed it at the boy. "You've got exactly five seconds to put down that bat and start walking back across the street," he said. "One ... two ..."

"He's got a piece, Dennis. Pop him."

Alan turned just in time to see the black boy pull out a handgun and fire through the closed passenger window. Glass shattered and Alan's right shoulder knotted with pain, forcing him to transfer the pistol to his left hand. He started to fire it at the boy, but something kept him from squeezing the trigger. The bullets had been meant for Jake Smyrna and for himself or for just Smyrna, depending on his final decision, which he had not yet made. One thing he did know now: he wasn't going to shoot anyone else, no matter what the provocation.

"Pop him again, Dennis. Give him one to remember us by."

There was another blast and this time Alan felt pain in his side, enough to make him cry out. His vision blurred.

"The motherfucker'll remember that one. Let's get the hell outta here, Snake."

As he lay slumped against the seat, Alan felt almost relieved, almost glad the decision he had wrestled with for so long had been taken out of his hands. He closed his eyes and thought of his wife and daughter, taking some solace in being on the verge of sharing with them the only thing the three of them could possibly share.

After a moment Kate and Mary Lilly faded from his consciousness, replaced by a young parishioner in his Chockoyotte congregation, a teen-age girl who had depended on him more even than had Miss Beck and Miss Sue.

"What gives you the right to quit and not me?" she asked, staring down at him.

Alan gave her the only answer he knew. "Because I lost my family ... and I no longer feel the same about God."

"You didn't give me the option of quitting when you helped me through my ordeal," she said. "And you didn't even bring God into it. You told me as long as there was one other person in this world who gave a rip whether I lived or died, I owed it to that person not to end my life. Were you lying, Mr. Buchannan?"

"That's what I believed at the time," he said and tried to banish her from his thoughts. But memory transported him back to Grace Episcopal Church in Chockoyotte, and he saw her kneeling at the communion rail, preparing to receive the cup which he handed her—Rhonda Selden, the daughter of Hal and Connie Selden who ran the local taxi service. Although her face had been hideously disfigured in the fire that nearly destroyed their home, she still had a lovely smile and the prettiest eyes imaginable.

"In time you'd have found someone else to sustain you," she said, handing him back the cup.

"I doubt it. But even if I had, there's more to it. There's Jake Smyrna."

"So what? Couldn't you have outlasted him? Couldn't you have found the courage to live through your anger and resentment like I found the strength to live through my despair?"

"I don't think so. I did what I had to do considering my limitations. I'm not as strong as you, Rhonda."

"You could have found the strength, Mr. Buchannan."

"How?"

"By coming to me. I could have given you what you needed just like you gave me what I needed."

She stood up and began to remove her clothes, revealing a body that filled him with desire. Her smile was gentle and her eyes full of love.

"I would have been yours for as long as you needed me ... forever if that's what you wanted."

When he reached out his hand to pull her close, there was no substance where her body should have been. And then she too faded from his consciousness.

Alan had only a moment to reflect on the import of her apparition before hearing footsteps. Opening his eyes, he saw Miss Beck moving as fast as she could toward his car.

"Are you all right, Mr. Buchannan? I heard what sounded like shots. Oh, my goodness, you've been hurt!"

With great effort Alan helped her open the door. He was both glad and ashamed when she put her arms around him and tried to comfort him. As he drifted toward oblivion, he squeezed her hand and did his best to leave her with a smile.

THE GOOD DOCTOR (2009)

Her second oxycodone of the day had just kicked in when Rhonda Selden got a call on her cell phone directing her to a fare at the county airport. "The guy was pissed he actually had to call for transportation," her mother, who was also Totem Taxi's dispatcher, told her. "His name is Winslow. Dr. Winslow. And he's in a hurry."

"Isn't everybody these days? Rush, rush, rush … people rushing their guts out and it's not even Thanksgiving yet. Where will I find this Dr. Winslow—inside the terminal, outside the terminal, or in the crapper?"

"He said he'll be waiting outside. You sound kinda weird, Rhonda. You're not high on something, are you?"

"Not me. I'm sharp as a tack and ready to roll. I'll check in after I deliver the good doctor to wherever the hell he's going."

When Rhonda arrived at the tiny airport, the only person waiting outside the terminal was a tall scowling young man with close-cropped red hair. She pulled to the curb and rolled down the window. "You need a taxi, mister?"

"It's about time you got here."

"Listen, bub. Someone I really liked died recently and I'm in no mood for any crap. You want a taxi or don't you?"

"Yeah, I do," the man said, some of the wind having left his sails. "I need to be at Chockoyotte's veterinary clinic at two o'clock. Is that a problem?"

Rhonda glanced at her watch. "Shouldn't be. Normally I'd load your suitcase for you, but if you want to save time, just toss it in the back seat and hop in."

The young man did as suggested and slid into the front seat opposite Rhonda.

"I'd appreciate it if you didn't stare at my face," she told him as she pulled away from the curb.

"Actually, I wasn't. I was admiring your figure."

"Yeah, put a bag over my head and I'm every man's dream."

"You sure are touchy. Maybe we ought to start over."

"Suit yourself."

He introduced himself as Peter Winslow, then said he had just graduated from the Virginia-Maryland Regional College of Veterinary Medicine. "I'm interviewing for Dr. Hux's old job. I understand he won't be a tough act to follow."

Rhonda barely slowed down for the stop sign at the entrance to Highway 158 before pulling into traffic and heading east. "Yeah? Why not?"

"Word has it he kept practicing too long. At least that's what the mayor told me on the phone the other day. Said he lost a lot of pets he shouldn't have."

"I wouldn't know about that. Personally I liked the man."

"You knew him?"

"Sort of."

"Tell me about him. I'd like to know about the guy I'm replacing ... assuming I decide to take the job."

Rhonda didn't feel much like talking, but she figured what the hell, it might not be a bad idea to focus for a while on something other than what happened to Cindy Laughton.

"The first time I met Dr. Hux was when I took a cat to his office," she said, pulling out to pass a dump truck loaded with gravel ...

"Are you familiar with the word responsibility*?" the old veterinarian asked, staring at her through glasses with lenses so thick they reminded her of two pop bottle bottoms.*

"Yeah, I know what it means."

"Then why did you wait until this cat is practically eaten up with tapeworm before bringing him in? Didn't you notice his sluggishness and lack of appetite? And how could you miss the worm segments around his anus?"

"To begin with, that cat's a stray my mom took in. And in the second place, even if he was mine, I wouldn't go around checking his butt all the time."

"His coat is a disgrace," Dr. Hux went on, unfazed

by Rhonda's attempt at sarcasm. *"Doesn't he get any attention at all?"*

"I didn't come in here for a lecture, Doc. All I want is ..."

"Young lady, do you know another veterinarian?"

"I know there's one in Roanoke Falls."

"There are two over there, both capable as far as I know. I'll be glad to refer you to one of them."

"That's too far to go just to have a cat checked out."

"Well, as long as you feel that way, you'll just have to put up with whatever I tell you. Now, if you and your mother had used common sense and exercised some responsibility, I wouldn't have had to tell you anything."

The young veterinarian wanted to know more about Dr. Hux, so Rhonda told him about the time she brought in a dog she happened to pass on the way back from Halifax, an old hound lying on the side of the road. After Dr. Hux realized nothing could be done for the dog, he spent a long time stroking his head and speaking soft words of affection before giving him the shot that put him down ...

"It was nice of you to bring him in, Miss Selden. Perhaps I underestimated you when you were here with your mother's cat. If so, I apologize. By the way, how's that cat doing?"

"Not too good, I'm afraid."

"What's wrong with him?"

"He died a few weeks ago."

"How?"

"Same way as that dog, I guess. I found him on the curb when I went out to get the morning paper."

"They don't have a chance, do they?"

"Beg your pardon?"

"The critters. If hunters don't kill them, careless drivers will. You should have kept that cat indoors where he'd be safe."

Rhonda started to take issue with that, but the old vet continued his diatribe before she could reply.

"Sometimes I wonder why I bother. I do everything I can to help the animals. I patch up their wounds. I treat their diseases. I plead with their owners to exercise good judgment and responsibility. What good does it do? Most of them end up victims of the busy monster manunkind."

"Victims of what?"

"It's a phrase in a poem I doubt you'd understand. No offense, Miss Selden. I just don't think Mr. Cummings would be your cup of tea."

"What's a poem got to do with my mom's cat anyway?"

"That cat had something precious until a careless human snatched it away: a life."

"It was probably an accident. They do happen, you know. Even people who care about animals have accidents. Most folks are decent enough if you give 'em half a chance. What about me? I stopped for that hound, didn't I?"

"Yes, you did. And I have no doubt you're a cut above the rest as far as human decency goes. Most people would have ignored that dog just as the priest and the Levite passed the wounded man on the other

side of the road."

"Oh, I don't know. I ..."

Dr. Hux waved away whatever she was going to say. "Spare me the platitudes about man's virtues, Miss Selden. The truth is the world is dominated by the ignorant and the inhumane. Mexico and Spain have their bullfights. Canada and Japan harvest seal pups. We Americans have our slaughter houses, testing labs, dog fights, rodeos, cock fights, and a plethora of insensitive pet owners. Cruelty to animals is our way of life." The old vet banged a fist against the table. "It galls me that I can't do a damn thing about it."

Rhonda started to tell him he ought to lighten up a little, maybe take a vacation or find himself a hobby, but she figured it would be a waste of breath. Dr. Hux wasn't going to listen to her or anybody else. Still she couldn't let him get away with what he'd just said. "Most people aren't cruel to animals," she told him. "I know I'm not, and neither are my mom and dad."

"By any chance is your father a hunter, Miss Selden?"

"He was before he had his stroke. Used to take me with him. Last time we went I bagged a six-point buck."

"And you're telling me you don't inflict pain and grief? What do you call killing a deer or a rabbit or a squirrel? Don't you realize they feel sadness when they lose a mate or an offspring or a parent? What is it but inflicting pain and grief when you shoot an animal?"

"If people didn't hunt, there'd be way too many animals," Rhonda replied. "A lot of 'em would starve to death."

"The same can be said of people. There are way too many of us. Why don't we have open season on human beings? Thinning our ranks would make it a lot more pleasant for those of us who survive, don't you think?"

"There's a big difference between animals and people, Doc."

"Of course there is. We should know better."

By that time Rhonda had had about all she could take of the man. "I gotta go pick up a fare."

"Don't go just yet," Dr. Hux said, his manner softening. "This isn't a bad conversation, even if we don't see eye to eye about things. What's your first name, Miss Selden?"

She told him, surprised that he wanted her to stay.

"There's a pot of coffee in my office, Rhonda. How about having a cup with me. We can talk about something else."

"Well ..."

"We'll talk about the weather or a book you might've read lately, anything that comes to mind. I rarely engage in a good conversation and I'd like to do more of it. Right now I feel an urge to sit down and have a cup of coffee with another human being—you, Rhonda ... even if you are a hunter."

About a mile from Chockoyotte the traffic picked up. When the highway added a third lane, Rhonda gunned the taxi around two slow-moving cars and in the process was able to slip through a yellow light on the verge of turning red.

"Nice move," the young vet said. "I might be on time after all. So what did you and the good doctor talk about?"

"Not much of anything."

"You must have talked about something."

"He asked how my dad was getting along and whether my mom and I would be able to make a go of the taxi business with him laid up. I asked Dr. Hux if he liked to fish."

"I think we better steer clear of that subject," the old veterinarian said. "Too close to what we were arguing about. Did your mother get another cat?"

"Not yet. I'm trying to convince her to try a dog this time."

Rhonda couldn't think of much else to say, and Dr. Hux seemed to have the same problem. After a while she thanked him for the coffee and got up to leave.

"Thank you for bringing in the dog," he said and shook her hand. "If more people were like you, maybe I wouldn't feel so ... so down on the human race."

"Did you have any more dealings with him after that?" the young vet asked.

Rhonda shook her head. "Our paths never crossed again."

"The mayor told me Dr. Hux went through a personality change the last year or so before he died. What was that all about?"

"I guess he started easing up on folks. He hardly said a word anymore about whether we were treating animals the way we should. My mom did get another cat, and when she took him in for shots, she couldn't believe the improvement in the doc's personality. Said he was downright personable."

The "Welcome-to-Chockoyotte" sign appeared on their right, and Rhonda slowed the taxi to forty-five miles an hour, ten miles faster than the posted speed limit. A moment later she wheeled into the veterinary clinic's parking area, stopping next to the only other vehicle in the gravel lot, an ancient-looking Chevy Prism with a cracked windshield.

"It's exactly one fifty-eight," she said, glancing at her watch, then at the meter. "Your fare is fifteen dollars and twelve cents. Make it fifteen bucks even. No charge for my conversation."

The young vet took out his wallet and handed her a ten-dollar bill and five ones. "I'll need a ride to the Holiday Inn after my interview. You'll get your tip when we get there."

"How long do you expect the interview to last?"

"A half hour should do it. The mayor pretty much said the job is mine if I want it. He wouldn't be driving that old clunker, would he?"

After Rhonda told him the Prism belonged to Leona Figgins, Dr. Hux's long-time assistant, the young vet said he might as well go have a chat with her. "Can I count on you being here when I come out?"

"I'll have to keep the meter running. It's fifty cents a minute when I wait. Half an hour will cost you an extra fifteen bucks."

"Don't expect a big tip."

Rhonda turned away, thoughts of Cindy once again uppermost in her mind. If only she hadn't introduced that girl to weed their senior year in high school ...

"What's the matter, kiddo? You look like you just

lost your last friend."

Winfield Barnes, Chockoyotte's long-time mayor, had driven up without Rhonda noticing. "Something like that," she said. "Dr. Winslow's inside."

"If you're waiting for him, you might as well join us. No reason to sit out here in the cold."

Rhonda didn't reply, but after a moment she decided she'd probably be better off being with other people than alone with thoughts of Cindy.

She followed the mayor into the building and watched him go over to where the young vet was talking to Leona Figgins and introduce himself. The two men chatted for a while and then Barnes suggested they take a stroll around the premises.

When they came to the kennels out back, he did a double take.

"Can't be. That dog's been dead for months. Died after I brought her in with the broken leg she got when my grandson dropped her off the porch. Darn kid wanted to see if she'd land on her feet like a cat."

As the mayor headed for the kennel to make sure it was the same dog, Rhonda noticed that Leona Figgins was biting her lip, as though trying to stifle a smile.

"It's Pepper all right," Barnes said. "She's still wearing that fancy collar my wife got her."

The black woman chuckled.

"What's so funny? You know something about this I don't?"

"Yes, sir, I do. Here everybody thought Dr. Hux was failing and couldn't do his job, and the fact is he'd been doing his job and a whole lot besides. The last year or so of his life, that man operated an underground railroad, one for pets. He told their owners, the ones he felt mistreated 'em, that they'd died. Then he took 'em out in the country or to other towns and gave 'em to people he knew would provide a decent home. We never got a chance to place Pepper."

The mayor and the young vet looked at each other as if they couldn't possibly believe such a tale. "Well, I don't know," Barnes said. "It might be like she says. But I wouldn't of thought even Dr. Hux crazy enough to pull a stunt like that."

For the first time in weeks Rhonda felt like laughing. Noticing that Dr. Winslow looked none too happy, she decided he must be wondering what sort of town Chockoyotte was or maybe what kind of person he'd become if he located there.

"Can't imagine there was much money in it," the mayor said, still looking perplexed.

Leona's smile dissolved. "He didn't do it for profit. Most of the time he paid folks to take 'em. I sent out checks every so often to pay for they keep."

Barnes nodded, as though he'd finally been able to take it all in and at least now could see the whole picture. "Why, that old fox. The personality change was part of his scheme, wasn't it? He acted all friendly and nice to divert suspicion away from what he was doing with people's pets."

Leona's face was as sober as the young vet's now, though in a different way, a sad sort of way. "That wasn't it at all. Once Dr. Hux figured out how to transfer pets from bad homes to good ones, well, I think it was like ... like finally, after all these years, he realized that folks were ... well, just folks, and there weren't any point staying mad at 'em."

"I still say it was to throw us off the scent."

Dr. Winslow took a step forward. "If you ask me, that old man wasn't playing with a full deck."

The mayor shrugged. "Can't argue with that. You don't act the way Dr. Hux did and not be at least a little touched in the head."

Rhonda went over and stood next to Leona. "He wasn't crazy," she said. "Dr. Hux might've seen things different from the way most people do, but he wasn't crazy."

"What riled you up all of a sudden?" Barnes asked. "This young man is entitled to his opinion, and so am I."

"That's true," Rhonda said, then added: "I'm sure you'll enjoy each other's company while you drive him to the Holiday Inn."

As she pulled out of the parking lot, Rhonda found herself thinking of the two-year program in substance-abuse counseling offered at the county community college, the only course of study she had ever seriously considered enrolling in—and then only during the brief periods when she actually thought she might be able to give up the substances. It's probably just a pipe dream, she was quick to remind herself. She'd had such dreams before, but like the early morning fogs that sometimes shut down the airport, they always dissipated within a few hours.

Maybe this time would be different, she told herself. If Dr. Hux could find the wherewithal to make such a drastic change in himself while at the same time going the extra mile for the animals, maybe she could do something with her life besides cart people's sorry asses around all day …

Two blocks from the veterinary clinic, she pulled over to the curb to let her mother know she was available for the next fare. While dialing Totem Taxi's number, she noticed that her throat felt parched and her temples were starting to throb, a sure sign her last oxycodone was beginning to wear off.

WELCOME TO THE NEIGHBORHOOD (2013)

The day after six white jurors let a guilty white man walk in Florida, thumbing their noses at black people in the process, our next-door neighbor called to say she and her husband couldn't come over for cards that night. She muttered something about Sam being under the weather and then she hung up. Since Sam had ignored me that morning when I spoke to him in the backyard, it didn't take an Einstein to suspect what ailed the man was his reaction to the verdict.

But I'm getting ahead of myself. To understand what's happening here, you need to know how much Chockoyotte has changed over the last sixty years or so. Back when I was growing up in the fifties, the town was segregated. Black people lived on the west side of the Atlantic Coast Line tracks in what was then known to most of us whites as colored town. We lived on the east side of the tracks, which is where the money also resided, not to mention the best business establishments and the nicest homes. The niggers, as some of us had the gall to call them then, would cross the tracks to get to work or to shop or occasionally just to hang out, but none of 'em lived over here. Now they pretty much live where they want to.

You probably think Carol and I have a problem with that. Well, we did consider moving to Roanoke Falls after learning that the Hartungs, our long-time next-door neighbors, were moving to an assisted-living facility over there and had sold their house to a black family. That news came as quite a shock.

When I asked Rogers, who had been Chockoyotte High's principal starting back when the school was all white, why he would do such a thing, he gave me the same kind of look he probably gave his teachers if they ever had the nerve to question him.

"Because Sam offered more than the other prospective buyers," he said without a hint of apology.

"Sam?" I said.

"Sam Hines. He works at Jamison Valve. One of the supervisors, I believe. He and his wife won't be a problem, Doug."

"That's easy for you to say. How would you have felt if Carol and I had moved out a few years ago and sold our house to a black family?"

"I wouldn't have liked it a damn bit. But I'd have accepted it. I'm sure in time you'll do the same."

I wasn't exactly pleased with Rogers' response but I let it go. The Hartungs had always been good neighbors, plus I'd long since reached the conclusion that black people had every right to live where they wanted. I just didn't particularly want them living next door to me.

The Hartungs held an estate sale before they moved, so they didn't have a lot of possessions to take with them. Their son lives in Rocky Mount, and he rented a small U-haul and moved all the heavy stuff in a single load. Their daughter lives in Roanoke Falls, and she helped with everything else, as did Carol and me. The entire move took less than three hours. There was a minimum of commotion.

The contrast couldn't have been greater when Sam and his wife moved in the following Saturday. One minute the neighborhood was peaceful and quiet without a black person in sight, and then here they come, like a swarm of locusts descending, enough of 'em to move ten families. The first thing they did was set up a picnic table in the side yard and start loading it up—sandwiches, fried chicken, potato salad, deserts, you name it. A black guy big enough to play tackle for the Charlotte Panthers unloaded a cooler full of beer from the back of a pickup truck. Another black dude wearing enough jewelry to stock a pawn shop set up a bunch of folding chairs, and a third carried a boom box over to the shade of a pecan tree and turned it on, blasting the neighborhood with rap. How anybody can call that stuff music is beyond me.

It was like a fourth of July picnic. Not long after the shindig started, a big U-haul backed into the Hartungs' driveway, the damn thing barely missing Carol's rose bushes. Some of the movers parked their vehicles at the edge of our property, which wouldn't have been a problem except a young black with shoulder-length dreadlocks used our yard to turn his motorcycle around in and left tire tracks on the lawn.

The move—or I should say festival—lasted most of the day, the boom box blaring the whole time. The neighborhood sounded like a rap concert. It looked like one too, reminding me of pictures of Woodstock except there wasn't a white face in the crowd. By mid-afternoon I'd had enough and drove down to the Shamrock. I had a couple beers and let off some steam, more than I should have I know, though not enough to get all the resentment out of my system. Before the move started, Carol and I had fully intended to go over and introduce ourselves to the new neighbors, but when I got back from the Shamrock, even though things had quieted down by then and all but two of the vehicles next door were gone, I wouldn't have welcomed those people to the neighborhood if they had been the Duke and Dutchess of Windsor.

The next morning I was working in my postage stamp of a vegetable garden pulling up weeds when I heard the back door of the Hartungs' house—I wished it was still their house—open and close. I didn't bother looking up and hoped whoever had stepped outside wouldn't notice me. Or if they did, they'd leave me the hell alone. No such luck.

"You know anything about that hate message my wife and I got last night?"

A large middle-aged black man was standing at the edge of my property. "Hate message?" I said as I stood up.

"Somebody spray-painted our front door. It said niggers aren't welcome in this neighborhood."

"Oh yeah? Did you report it to the sheriff?"

"I did. He said there's nothing he can do without a witness. I was hoping you might've seen or heard something."

I shook my head. "Sorry."

He looked at me as though sizing me up. Finally he let out a sigh of resignation. "Sam Hines," he said, extending his right arm over the chicken wire fence that enclosed my garden.

I gave him a dead fish of a shake, the kind I don't like getting myself. "Doug Courtright."

"You used to be the sheriff."

It wasn't a question but I nodded anyway. "Been retired going on three years now."

"You don't look old enough."

"I'll be sixty-eight my next birthday."

"You've kept yourself in good shape."

He was trying to be friendly but I was in no mood to reciprocate. I glanced at the pile of weeds I'd accumulated, hoping he'd take the hint.

"Nice garden," he said. "I always wanted one but never had the space."

"Well, now you do." The tone of my voice wouldn't even have registered on the friendly scale.

He looked away, shifting weight from one foot to the other. "Doug, I'd like to apologize for all the racket yesterday," he said, re-establishing eye contact. "I don't particularly like big gatherings myself, and I definitely don't like loud music. But it's hard to ask folks to turn down the volume when they've given up their Saturday to help you move."

I nodded, surprised by the apology but not quite

willing to accept it. Sam wished me a good day and went back to his house. I decided I'd done enough weeding for one day and went back to mine.

The next day Carol made a batch of wine jelly, one of her specialties. It's not the kind you put on toast or crackers like a lot of people seem to think but a dessert that contains a small amount of sherry wine and has the consistency of Jello. She took a bowl of it next door and stayed longer than I expected. When she got home, she reported that Sam's wife Belinda had a passion for antiques that rivals her own and a collection of vintage costume jewelry that put hers to shame. She said the two of them planned to attend an estate sale in Roanoke Falls later in the week, an announcement she was more pleased to make than I was to hear.

Sam's passion turned out to be golf. One afternoon when we both happened to be in our respective yards, he offered to teach me how to play. I told him I never could see much point in chasing after a little white ball. Besides, I said, I couldn't afford a country club membership even if I wanted one. Not a problem, he said. If I'd learn the basics of the game, he'd take me with him to the public course he plays near Emporia. I said I'd think about it.

That night somebody threw a rock with a note attached through Sam's living room window. He told me about it the next morning, said it happened about two AM. The note said if he and Belinda didn't come to their senses and move back across the tracks where they belong they'll wish to hell they had.

"We didn't see who did it, but he drove what looked

like a subcompact and it's got a noisy muffler. The deputy I reported it to said they'd look into it. That was about eight hours ago and so far nobody's come by to check out the damage. Belinda can't take much more of this, Doug. I hate to ask you but is there some way you can light a fire under our current sheriff?"

I told him Marvin Tucker and I had never particularly hit it off and I doubted I'd have much influence with him.

"Then don't worry about it," Sam said. "At least we've got you and Carol next door. When you were sheriff you had a reputation for being fair with black folks, which is one reason Belinda and I bid as high as we did on that house. It's a good feeling knowing you're just a stone's throw away."

I didn't know if Sam was trying to tell me something or not with that reference to a stone, but it didn't really matter. It was what he said about being fair to black people that got my attention.

I started to tell him I knew who was behind the harassment—at least I thought I did—and I'd see if I could put a stop to it. Knowing Sam, he would have wanted to know the specifics, so I just told him to hang in there and maybe things would cool down. I figured what he didn't know wouldn't hurt him—or me.

A few months passed without any more racial incidents, thanks to a talk I had with a guy I commiserated with at the Shamrock the afternoon of the move, a bigoted sort who drives a Mini Cooper that needs a new muffler. Hardly a weekend goes by that Carol and Belinda don't head off together in search of the ultimate garage sale. When Carol found out that

Belinda and Sam like to play cards, she suggested we invite them over for an evening of poker and blackjack. I tried to nix the idea but eventually she wore me down.

We didn't hear from Sam or Belinda for a few days after she cancelled out of the card game. Then one morning I was out picking squash and heard their back door open and close. It was Sam and he was heading in my direction.

"What did you think of the verdict?" he asked in a casual tone, though I could sense tension behind his words.

"What verdict?"

"The Zimmerman trial." He spoke the words like he might have been referring to a piece of carrion so disgusting a buzzard wouldn't touch it.

I shrugged. "That's what can happen when there's a stand-your-ground law on the books."

"We've got a law like that in this state."

"I know we do."

"You think it's a good law?"

I shook my head. "Actually I don't."

"Why not?"

I didn't know why Sam was grilling me, though I had an idea. I set the bag of squash on the ground, looked him in the eye, and said what to me and Carol was obvious. "That black kid was minding his own business. He had a right to be where he was."

"His name is Travon Martin."

"I know that. I also know he was stalked and harassed and ultimately shot simply because he was black and wearing a hoodie."

Sam looked at me like he thought I might be bullshitting him. "But you'd still have voted *not guilty* if you'd been on that jury, wouldn't you, Doug?"

I shook my head. "The guy got away with murder, Sam. Those Florida jurors should be ashamed of themselves."

"Amazing," he muttered after a moment.

"What is?"

"That you'd see it that way ... especially after the welcome-to-the-neighborhood you gave Belinda and me. It was you behind that racial shit at my house, wasn't it?"

I didn't see that one coming. My first impulse was to deny it, but I decided I owed Sam the truth. "I wasn't exactly behind it," I said. "But I'm not exactly blameless either." I explained how angry I was at him and his movers for acting like they owned the neighborhood and how I went to the Shamrock and did some venting. "One guy there really lapped it up. He said you should be taught a lesson and he just might be the person to do it. He's a known blow-hard, so I didn't take him seriously until you told me about the spray painting. I thought it would end there. When it didn't, I had a talk with him. I told him you'd turned out to be a good neighbor and if anything else like that happened at your place, I'd report him as a hate-crime perpetrator and testify against him at the trial. I overreacted about the noise, Sam. I'm sorry about that. And I should have kept my mouth shut at the Shamrock."

He took a moment to process what I'd just said, and then without saying anything he turned and walked back to his house. The back door slammed behind him.

We didn't see Sam or Belinda for the next two days. On the third day I was out picking tomatoes when their back door opened and out comes Sam. I glanced up long enough to make sure he wasn't carrying a weapon of some sort, and then I resumed my picking. He stood next to my garden and waited until I gave him my full attention.

"Why the hell did you wait so long to explain things?" he asked, sounding more frustrated than angry.

"I didn't want you knowing I was part of it," I told him. "I was afraid you'd hold it against me."

"Is that so?"

I nodded. "I apologized, Sam. There's not much else I can do."

He gazed off into the distance, seemed to be trying to figure out what to say or do next. Finally he nodded, like a judge who's made up his mind but you don't know yet the nature of his verdict.

"You probably don't recall me saying it, Doug, but a while back I complimented this garden of yours."

"Yeah, I remember."

"Well, I was lying. Fact is this garden is pitiful. It's downright pathetic. There's no sweet corn, no butter beans, no field peas, no string beans. I don't even see any onions in there."

"A garden big enough to grow all that stuff would take up my whole yard," I said, wondering what possessed Sam to go off on such a tangent.

"Not necessarily. We put our minds to it, we could have a real garden out here, half on your property and half on mine. That way we'd both have something to be proud of, not to mention a whole lot of good eating.

And it wouldn't mess up either of our yards. Something to consider for next spring, don't you think?"

I looked at him like he'd lost his mind. But the more I considered the idea, the less ridiculous it seemed. "You're not bullshitting me, are you, Sam?"

"Nope. Seems doable to me. What you say, Doug? You interested or not?"

I looked at his yard and then at mine, trying to visualize exactly where such a garden would go and how much of an eyesore it would be. "Carol will probably object on aesthetic grounds."

"What if she doesn't?"

"If she doesn't ... well, in that case ... maybe I'll take you up on it. But on one condition."

"What's that?"

"Once the damn thing is planted, I get to do at least half the work. That's only fair since I'm the one retired."

He gave me a cockeyed look. "You'll get to do *exactly* half the work," he said in a prickly tone, though I thought I detected the trace of a smile on his face. "Gotta watch you white folks like a hawk. Give you an inch and you'll take a mile."

I didn't know how to respond to that. "Sometimes I think you're full of shit, Sam," I finally said and stuck out my hand. "If Carol agrees to the arrangement, you've got yourself a deal."

HARVEY'S COUP (2016)

The van roared up behind the Chevy Spark, veered around it, then swerved back across the right lane just in time to take the exit ramp. "Screw you," said Harvey Driscol in response to the flurry of honking that followed, sounding to him more like the calls of a sick duck than a horn. "You don't piddle along on an interstate and expect not to get sucked up somebody's tailpipe. Besides, if you had two nickels to rub together, you wouldn't be driving that cheap piece of crap."

At the bottom of the ramp, Harvey slowed for the stop sign—he never actually stopped for one unless a cop was in view, and he had contempt for people who did. Turning to the left, he passed the Holiday Inn where he had stayed five years earlier and planned to stay tonight, and crossed under the interstate, heading east toward Chockoyotte, hoping he would have better luck there than he'd had anywhere else on this fiasco of a buying trip. During the past three days, he had attended a host of estate sales, antique malls, flea markets, garage sales, and even two auctions, but he hadn't executed a single coup. He thought he had one yesterday after buying a red Carnival glass bowl, but last night in his motel room in Richmond, he noticed the damn thing had a crack. He'd been snookered—by a flea market dealer no less—and all because he'd been in such a hurry to get to an auction where his only purchases had been a common pattern glass bowl and one lousy string of Indian trading beads.

It still might be possible to get big bucks for the Carnival piece, but Harvey knew he'd have to be extremely lucky. In perfect condition it was worth about five hundred dollars because of its rare red color. He'd put four-ninety on it and let some sucker bargain him down to four-fifty. If the sucker ended up returning it, Harvey would first try to convince him in a pleasant way that the bowl hadn't been cracked when it left the shop, and if that didn't work, he'd say "Sue me."

The problem, though, was that suckers, both buyers and sellers, were becoming a rare breed. Everyone who came in his shop these days seemed to be armed with a magnifying glass and information gleaned from various antique publications on how not to get taken by a dealer. The sellers too were more knowledgeable. Every Tom, Dick, and Billy Bob had price guides or had checked on ebay to see what items were going for, which made it next to impossible to get valuable antiques for a steal. This trip in particular had made

Harvey remember with fondness the days when people were happy to get rid of their old stuff, antiques included, for whatever they could get for it. Nowadays they would put big dollars on a cow pie if it looked more than a few days old.

Even the prostitutes on this trip had been outrageously high. Last night in Richmond, Harvey had pulled up beside a slightly plump one whose looks he liked, and when she said her price was a hundred and fifty dollars, he almost fell out of his van. When he offered her seventy-five, she laughed. "Guess I'll keep looking until I find somebody that doesn't charge by the pound," he told her, and drove back to the motel where he called his wife and complained bitterly about how prices on everything had skyrocketed out of control.

At the outskirts of Chockoyotte, he began to experience the exhilaration he always felt when the possibility of swinging a deal was imminent. He accelerated and blew past a pickup truck, pulling back into the right lane just in time to avoid an oncoming Pontiac with a blaring horn.

"Try your wipers, Leroy," he said with a chuckle. "I see you're into antiques too. You're driving one."

At Washington Avenue, which he recognized as the street he wanted, he turned right and headed south. He had been to Chockoyotte once before on a successful stock replenishment trip, having bought a batch of Carnival glass at a good price in addition to pulling off a truly magnificent coup. Be just my luck they've croaked, he thought. "Lord," he said, glancing toward the van's roof, "how about giving ole Harv a break for a change. Let those old codgers still be alive and in business and cut me one more sweet deal before they shuffle off to that glorious antique mall in the sky."

Al and Sadie's Antiques & Junque was still there, an old two-story frame house just inside the town limits and directly across the street from a pile of rubble Harvey thought he remembered as being a combination gas station and convenience store. Parking behind a brown van at least a decade older than his, he hoped the conglomeration of kitschy lawn ornaments in the front yard—deer, bears, roosters, squirrels, blond-haired Dutch boys, ornate birdbaths, and two black lawn jockeys—wasn't indicative of what he'd find inside.

When he opened the front door, his fears were confirmed. Al and Sadie were still alive, looking not much older than he remembered, but their shop was a disaster. Junk was everywhere—bottles, plates, bowls, odds and ends from china sets, reproduction Depression glass. One whole table was filled with used books and magazines, another with toys more battered than old, a third with mass-produced wooden birdhouses and mailboxes. The walls were covered with gaudy velvet paintings in cheap plastic frames.

"What happened?" Harvey asked, walking over to the counter where the old man was tinkering with a Seth Thomas clock, the only item he'd seen so far that qualified as an antique. "Last time I was here you had some quality merchandise."

"Still do," Al said, looking a little irritated. "Most of the antiques are in the other rooms. When was you here last?"

"About five years ago. I bought a batch of Carnival

glass."

Al's eyes narrowed. "I thought I recognized you. We gave you a good deal on that Carnival, and then you had the gall to cheat us out of our Stangl bird."

Damn, Harvey thought. They found out what that bird was really worth. "I didn't cheat you out of anything. We agreed on a price and I paid it."

"I told you at the time we hadn't had a chance to research that bird. You swore on your honor as a fellow dealer that it was a common piece. Turned out it was rare as hen's teeth."

"I didn't know it was valuable until I got home and my wife checked it out on the internet."

Sadie, who was hunched over a roll-top desk near the end of the counter when Harvey came in, was now glaring at him. "Did it ever occur to you to bring that bird back?" she asked. "Or maybe send us some of the profit you made?"

Harvey shook his head. "I don't know any dealer who'd have done that. Windfalls are part of the business, ma'am. I'm sure you've had your share."

"We've had a hard time making ends meet the last few years," Sadie replied. "We really could've used the money from that Stangl bird."

"Well, if it's any consolation to you, I got taken myself just yesterday. I paid two hundred and fifty dollars for a red Carnival glass bowl, and it turned out to be cracked. I'll be lucky to get twenty bucks for the darn thing."

Actually he had paid seventy-five dollars for the bowl, but since it was still possible he would end up buying more antiques from these people, assuming they had any, it was to his advantage if they thought of him more in terms of a fellow victim than as a victimizer.

"But you'll try to get a lot more, won't you?"

"Well, sure. That's the name of the game, isn't it, buy cheap and sell dear? But that doesn't mean I'd lie to a customer or someone I was buying from. If a person asks me the condition of an item, I tell him ... to the best of my knowledge at the time. Mind if I look in your other rooms?"

"Go ahead," Al said. "But don't expect to get anything for the kind of prices you paid last time."

There were three other rooms in the downstairs portion of the house, all containing various types of collectibles. Though few of the items were desirable, Harvey did find some he liked: a cut-glass bowl, three Czechoslovakian vases, two perfume bottles, and an Italian paperweight. He took them into the main part of the store and placed them next to the cash register.

"Got any more stock like this upstairs?" he asked the old couple, both of whom were now standing behind the counter.

"None that's for sale," Al said. "That's our living quarters up there."

"Then these are the items I'm interested in. Asking price comes to a grand total of two hundred and twenty-nine dollars. I'll give you a hundred and seventy-five for the lot."

"No sale. We'll take the full amount, two hundred and twenty-nine dollars ... assuming you added right."

"You got to be kidding. Nobody expects to get their asking price."

"I do—from you. You hoodwinked us once. You

won't do it again."

"I'll make it an even two hundred. No, I'll do better than that. I'll split the difference with you. I'll give you two hundred and five."

"Read my lips—two twenty-nine."

"Don't be foolish, Al," Sadie said. "His last offer seems fair enough for what he's buying."

"It would be if somebody else was buying it. But he owes us considerable from last time. If he don't want to pay our asking price, he can take his business elsewhere."

Harvey smiled. "You've got granite in your spine, Al ... or maybe in your head. I haven't run into such a stubborn cuss in years. How about two-twenty? That's my final offer. Nobody else would pay that much."

"Maybe not but nobody else walked out of here with our Stangl bird five years ago and paid next to nothing for it. Two twenty-nine. And if you keep on dickering, the price'll go up."

"For goodness sakes, Al, give it to him for two-twenty. We can't pay the bills with foolish pride."

"Stay out of this, Sadie. This is my transaction."

"But he's offered us a good price."

"Not good enough. Now go get supper started."

Sadie stared at her husband for a moment before turning away. "Pride goeth before a fall," she said as she hurried from the room.

"OK, Al, you win. I'll give you the two twenty-nine." Though he hated to pay anyone's asking price, Harvey didn't feel too bad. Since all the items were reasonably priced to begin with, he'd still be able to turn a nice profit.

"Not until I add them up." Al reached under the counter for a pad and pencil.

"Maybe you should check my pockets too. Some of that small treacle could've decided it wanted a change of scene."

"Two twenty-nine it is," Al said, ignoring the sarcasm. "Plus tax. Cash only. I don't accept checks."

"No tax." Harvey took out his wallet. "I've got a dealer number, remember?" He held out his card and waited while Al wrote down the number. Then he counted out the money and handed it over. "Better make sure it's not counterfeit. I'd sure hate for you to get snookered a second time."

"So you did know what the Stangl bird was worth."

"Not really. I figured I'd be able to sell it for a hundred bucks."

"Seems to me you told us forty dollars."

Harvey shrugged. "You tell the whole truth in this business, Al, you wind up broke. Maybe that's your problem."

"How much did you get for it?"

"Twelve hundred dollars," Harvey said, unable to resist revealing such a magnificent accomplishment.

Al shook his head and heaved a weary sigh. "Oh, well. Guess that's water over the dam ... unfortunately a hell of a lot of water. I'll pack up your purchases and help you take 'em to your van. Unlike some people, I still feel an obligation even after the sale."

"How'd you know I'm driving a van?"

"I looked. Business must be booming if you can afford nice wheels like that."

"Actually it's not. Running an antique business is a

lot tougher than it used to be."

"Reckon I know that better than you. You saw what this place was like five years ago, and you can see what it's like today."

"The whole town looks like it's gone downhill. What happened?"

"The blacks have pretty much taken over. A lot of white folks have moved out."

"Maybe you folks should do the same."

"Can't afford to. We couldn't buy much more than a shanty over in Roanoke Falls or anywhere else for what we could get for this place now."

Maybe if you had a little more taste and took the trouble to check out what you did have, Harvey felt like saying, you wouldn't have ended up in a house that looks like a Salvation Army depot.

A few minutes later he unlocked his van and swung open the side door. "Right there behind the seat will be fine, Al."

The old man put the box on the floor, then gazed at the accumulation of antiques and collectibles in the van. "Nice haul."

"I've done a lot better in years past," Harvey replied, surveying his purchases.

The van was nearly full. He had bought several big items this trip—chairs and tables and such—and they took up a lot of space. Near the back, however, was a small open area which he suddenly realized how he might fill. Although he would never allow such monstrosities near his own shop, he knew a flea market dealer who liked kitsch and was willing to pay top dollar for it. "How much you want for those artificial niggers?"

"Two hundred dollars," Al said after a brief hesitation.

"For the two of them?"

"Apiece."

"Forget it. I didn't realize they were solid gold."

Harvey had just started to climb into his van when he heard a door slam and saw Sadie shuffling across the yard.

"Would you be interested in this?" she asked, handing him a round object.

It was a Perthshire paperweight. "Sure. How much you asking for it?"

"I'll let you have it for forty dollars."

"It's not for sale," Al said brusquely. "Take it back in the house."

"No, it's mine. If I can get a reasonable price, I intend to sell it."

"Woman, we're not so hard up you've got to start selling off your own paperweights."

"Go look at our bank statement and this month's bills and tell me how well off we are, Al."

"Doesn't matter what we owe. I don't want you selling anything from your own collection ... especially to him."

"A while ago when you were doing the selling you told me to butt out. Now I'd like you to do the same."

The old man looked astonished. "I won't forget this, Sadie," he said, sounding more hurt than angry. "I don't care now if you sell him your whole goddamn collection. I'm going downtown and look for some decent company."

"Don't go to the Shamrock," she pleaded.

"That's exactly where I'm going." Al strode across the yard, glancing over his shoulder when he reached the decaying sidewalk. "I'll come home when I get good and ready. If it's dark and I'm still not back, you can eat supper without me."

With sad eyes the woman watched her husband walk away. Then she turned to Harvey. "I've got three more upstairs I'd like to sell. If you're agreeable, I'd just as soon make it a package deal."

A half hour later, an ecstatic Harvey Driscol drove slowly, even cautiously, through downtown Chockoyotte, having decided he'd check out the rest of the town before heading over to the Holiday Inn. There were few traffic lights and only two stop signs, one of which he actually stopped for, motioning to a couple of black kids on bicycles that he was giving them the right of way.

As he passed the Shamrock, a seedy-looking bar next to Wilson's Cafe, Harvey felt a twinge of remorse. Hell, it's not like I cheated them, he told himself. I paid his asking price, and I almost paid hers. Convinced by his own argument, he felt his guilt recede and finally disappear, a tiny boat lost on the sea of his delight at having accomplished what he'd thought impossible—turning this heretofore dismal buying trip into a resounding success.

The second and third paperweights Sadie had shown him were similar to the first, nice pieces but nothing special. Together they would probably bring a hundred and twenty-five dollars in his shop. The last paperweight, however, had almost taken his breath away. It was a Baccarat millefiori with Gridel silhouette canes, signed and dated B1848! He had seen a similar one sell at an auction for seventeen hundred dollars.

"I'll take a hundred and thirty-five dollars for the four," the old woman said. "I know they're worth more, but I didn't pay much for 'em and we need the cash."

"I'll give you a hundred and ten," Harvey said, trying to conceal his pleasure. "Keep in mind I've already bought a pile of stuff from you folks today and I paid your asking price. I'm not about to do something foolish like that again."

"A hundred and twenty-five," she countered.

"Make it a hundred and twenty and you've got yourself a deal."

Having seen all he wanted to of Chockoyotte, Harvey headed for the Holiday Inn. After crossing a set of railroad tracks and driving beneath a trestle with CSX painted on the side, he began to pick up speed, anxious to get to the motel where he could call his wife and tell her the news. A Baccarat millefiori with Gridel silhouette canes—and it had cost him next to nothing! He still could hardly believe it.

Glancing in his rear-view mirror for a last glimpse of Chockoyotte, a town for which he had acquired an affection in spite of its decrepit condition, he noticed a solitary vehicle on the road behind him. It looked like a van, a brown van. Don't tell me the old coot has already found out about the paperweights and is coming to rescue them, he thought, feeling a surge of anxiety. Harvey accelerated and the van fell behind. If that is him, he'll play hell catching me once I get on the interstate. I'll leave that rattletrap of his like it was standing still.

About a half mile from the interstate, after the road had straightened out, Harvey checked his mirror again. Seeing nothing but empty pavement, he felt foolish for having imagined the old man was following him. He's probably in his cups by now anyway, he thought, and wouldn't know whether they were Wedgwood or Spode.

Harvey wondered why Al had asked so much for the lawn jockeys. Even in the Baltimore area where he lived, they didn't cost that much, and everything else in the shop had been reasonably priced. Strange old birds, he reflected, and couldn't help chuckling. You'd think they would have learned their lesson the first time, and here they let me slip away with an even bigger coup.

"What the hell is that?" he muttered. Glancing around, he saw nothing unusual. No boxes had fallen or, as far as he could tell, even shifted positions. The Art Deco curio cabinet, the object for which he had paid the most on this trip, was still securely wrapped in blankets and hadn't moved. Everything appeared to be exactly as he had packed it.

He heard the noise again, a low rustling sound. Had an animal somehow scurried into the van, a cat or dog or maybe a squirrel? Such an occurrence didn't seem likely because he always kept the doors shut and locked. Had there been an instance lately when he hadn't locked the van's doors and had left it unattended? With a shock of fright Harvey realized that there had—when he returned to the house with Sadie to look at the rest of her paperweights.

"This here pistol aimed at your head ain't no antique," a familiar voice said. "And neither are the bullets in the chamber. Now slow down and keep your eyes on the road. There's a crossroads up ahead. I want you to take a right when we get there."

Midnight found the lights still on in Al and Sadie's bedroom. The old couple had worked hard all evening bringing in their new stock, arranging and rearranging it, carrying some of it upstairs where it would be stored until needed.

"Do you think it's possible he really didn't know the value of that Stangl bird?" Sadie asked as she sat at the dressing table brushing her hair with her newly-acquired antique silver brush.

"Hell, no," Al said, pulling back the covers and climbing into bed. "When they handed out scruples, that guy was standing in some other line."

"You know, I almost gave him a chance to redeem himself. I came real close to telling him I wasn't sure what that Baccarat was worth. Then, if he'd been honest with me, I might not have gone through with our plan."

"I'm glad you stuck to it. Far as I'm concerned, he got what he deserved. He'd just as soon steal us blind as look at us. He proved that twice."

"You're probably right. How'd he take it, Al?"

"You mean when he realized it was all over?"

"Yes."

"I expected him to whine and plead but he didn't. He just acted kind of stunned, like he couldn't believe what was happening."

About three miles northeast of Chockoyotte and about a mile from the interstate, a series of bubbles broke the surface of a remote gravel pit pond. They glinted in the moonlight like shards of cut glass—or a string of antique beads held high by some unseen auctioneer attempting to exhort from a reluctant crowd just one more best and final bid.

The March (2020)

On a hot Saturday morning in late August, approximately sixty people, almost all of them black, gathered in the parking lot of what once had been Chockoyotte's train station, a building that had served both the Seaboard and the Atlantic Coast Line railroads but was now the town library. The reason for the gathering would have been unthinkable four months earlier.

"Better line up," Sam Hines, the protest's coordinator, called out after glancing at his watch. "Remember, this is to be a peaceful march. No violence of any kind. And don't forget to wear your Covid masks. Belinda has some extras in case you need one."

"I still say we oughta pay our due respects to Colonel Cracker," said a young black man who wore a Colin Kaepernick jersey and held up his "No Justice No Peace" sign for emphasis. "We don't want that guy feelin' left out."

Sam shook his head. "We put that idea to bed at our last meeting, Jerome. The message we want to get across today is *Black Lives Matter*, period. Destruction of property will play into the hands of our enemies, especially that big racist in the White House. We need him out of there, which means we gotta be smart about the way we go about our business."

At Wednesday night's meeting, the final one of several held in the basement of Chockoyotte's African Methodist Episcopal Church, a few of the more militant attendees had suggested a change in the march's itinerary. Instead of heading west on Montgomery Street after the marchers passed the high school, they would first head east to the intersection of Sycamore and Cedar streets where the bronze stature of Colonel Patterson stood atop a granite pedestal. Once the marchers reached the statue, those who wished to participate would pull it down and make sure it never again functioned as an insult to black people. Cooler heads had prevailed, though, the vast majority of prospective marchers voting that the demise of Colonel Cracker, as they tended to call him, should at least wait until after the upcoming election.

Another issue the march's participants had discussed at a previous meeting was the specific nature of the signs and placards they would carry. Some thought that since the catalyst for their protest had been George Floyd's murder, they should limit the wordage to "Black Lives Matter," "Remember George Floyd," "I Can't Breathe," and whatever might pertain to other black victims of police violence such as Brianna Taylor, Eric Garner, John Crawford III, and Michael

Brown. In the end, however, the group decided that signs making reference to black people such as Emmitt Till and Travon Martin, victims of racism but not police violence, would also be appropriate, as would most any heartfelt words or phrases pertaining to systemic racism.

The placards carried by retired sheriff Doug Courtright and his wife, two of the handful of white people waiting for the march to begin, said "Hate Has No Place in Chockoyotte," a variation of the wording on the sign standing next to the "Biden for President" sign in their front yard. When Sam Hines, the Courtrights' next-door neighbor, asked if they would like to participate in the march, Doug and his wife had readily agreed but only after Sam assured them the protest would be strictly non-violent.

"Even if it's peaceful, there's bound to be pushback," Doug had warned. "If not from people here in town, then from some in Roanoke Falls. There's a lot more Trump signs over there than Biden signs."

"Hopefully the fact that you and Carol are marching with us will minimize that pushback," Sam had replied.

"Don't count on it. Times have changed since I was sheriff, and not necessarily for the better."

The march began as planned at ten AM, the marchers singing Kendrick Lamar's "Alright" as they crossed the spur track connecting the old Seaboard tracks to the switchyard now used by CSX. They had practiced that rap song, along with Janelle Monae's "Hell You Talmbout" and the gospel song "Ain't Gonna Let Nobody Turn Me 'Round" at their previous meetings.

The March went smoothly for the first twenty minutes or so as the participants worked their way through downtown Chockoyotte, turning left at Second Street, right on Sycamore Street, right again at Third Street, and then another left that put them back on Washington Avenue heading south. As expected, the small turnout of observers and will wishers consisted mostly of black people, but there were whites in attendance. A few even held up "Black Lives Matter" signs and shouted words of encouragement such as "We're with you!" and "Black lives do matter!" as the marchers passed. A young white woman with a face disfigured by burn marks held up a handwritten sign that said "With you all the way, my black brothers and sisters."

It wasn't until the marchers finished singing their version of "Hell You Talmbout" and were approaching the Route 258 intersection that Doug Courtright realized the pushback he predicted had already begun. A group of about fifteen white men of various sizes and ages, all dressed in camouflage clothing, had gathered on the west side of the intersection. One of them carried a Confederate flag; one an American flag; one a red, white and blue "Trump for President" flag; and one a sign that said "Blue Lives Matter." The rest of the men cradled rifles in their arms. None of them wore a mask.

"I hate to say I was right," Doug called out to Sam Hines, who was marching in a small group ahead of him. "But there's trouble waiting up at the corner."

"I see 'em," Sam replied. "We'll just have to ignore 'em and keep on marchin'."

By the time the lead group of marchers reached the intersection, however, the white counter-protestors had fanned out across Washington Avenue, forming a barricade.

"Nice mornin' for a walk," one of the men holding a rifle said in a mock friendly tone. "Where y'all headed?"

"That's our business," Sam replied, stepping forward. "We got a permit for this march."

The white man chuckled. "That and a dollar might get you a cup of coffee at Levi Wilson's joint. You folks would be welcome there." The man paused, shifting his rifle to a more comfortable position. "I take it you're the spokesman for this raggedy-assed group. What's your name?"

"Sam."

"You wouldn't happen to be headed for that statue of Colonel Patterson, would you, Sam?"

"Nope. We're not going anywhere near there."

"No? Something about that statue you don't like?"

"You might say that."

"We wouldn't want anything happening to that monument. And just to make sure it doesn't, these men and me, we're going to accompany you and the rest of these protestors for the duration of your march. How's that grab you, Sam?"

There were rumblings among the protestors, angry murmurs that concerned Sam almost as much as what the white man had just said. "That's a bad idea. A really bad idea."

"Well, we like it, and we're committed to it. Just think of us as protection. Nobody's going to mess with you people as long as we're with you. What do you say, Sam? It wouldn't hurt to have a few more white faces in the crowd, would it?"

The murmuring behind Sam grew louder, more angry, and for a moment he didn't know how to respond. The last thing he wanted was to let these bigoted yahoos have their way. But unless he did, there inevitably would be violence, something almost as bad as giving in to them.

"You can come with us if you leave your guns and two of those flags behind," he finally said. "And you'll all have to put on Covid masks."

The white man laughed. "Now why would you go and make such a ridiculous demand as that? It would be like us asking you to cancel this stupid march of yours. Which might not be a bad idea, now that I think about it. How 'bout it, Sam? If you and the rest of these misguided protesters turn around and go back home, it'll save y'all a lot of grief."

"Forget it. That's not going to happen."

The white man shrugged. "So where does that leave us, mister protest leader?"

Sam glanced at the protestors behind him as though for guidance, noticing that Doug Courtright had set his placard down and was leaning over, his back turned, and seemed to be talking on his cell phone. "You tell me."

"It leaves you with a choice. Either you agree to let us march right along with you or you'll have to fight your way past us. It's as simple as that. Maybe you'd like to confer with that old washed-up sheriff, get a white man's opinion on what you oughta do. Though if you ask me, he really isn't much of a man, taking sides with the likes of you."

What have I gotten us into? Sam wondered. And what can I do about it other than tell this shithead to go piss up a rope? The volume of disgruntled sounds behind him reaching an angry crescendo, he was about to do exactly that when he noticed Doug Courtright step forward.

"I just reported what's going on here to the State Highway Patrol," Doug said, holding up his cell phone. "A contingent of state troopers are on their way. If you people want to stick around and get arrested for harassment, that's up to you. In the meantime, those of us participating in this non-violent march will stay right where we are. At least that would be my advice. Sam and the rest of the marchers don't have to take it."

"Sounds like good advice to me," Sam said. "And while we're waiting, we can make good use of our time by singing another protest song." He turned and faced the marchers. "I've got one in mind, but I'm open to suggestions."

"Ain't Gonna Let Nobody Turn Me 'Round," shouted several of the marchers, and Sam, smiling now, nodded in agreement.

But the counter-protesters weren't done yet. As soon as the marchers began singing, the white men launched into a frenzied rendition of "Dixie." Both sides kept raising their voices until they were practically shrieking at each other. Finally the noise subsided, and for a long moment the two groups stood in silence glaring at each other. Eventually the silence was broken by the distant wail of an approaching siren.

"Nice meeting with y'all," the leader said as he turned to go, motioning for his men to follow. "Let's do it again sometime." Looking directly at Doug Courtright, he added, "We owe you one, nigger lover."

Late that night Sam Hines stood next to the vegetable garden he and his wife shared with the Courtrights. It was too dark to distinguish one plant from another, the moon having slipped behind a thick bank of clouds. But Sam knew they were there—collards, okra, squash, peppers, snap beans, cucumbers, field peas, plus all the vegetables needed for Brunswick stew: sweet corn, butter beans, yellow onions, tomatoes, and white potatoes. There was even a small watermelon patch—and most everything seemed to be thriving. Some mighty fine eating lay ahead.

For the past several minutes, Sam had been thinking about what happened at the Black Lives Matter march. He had mixed feelings about it, glad they had been able to complete the march but disappointed in the small turnout and the fact that the counter protestors had given them such a hard time. He tried to take consolation in the way people all over the country, both black and white, had responded to George Floyd's murder. What had really surprised him was the outrage exhibited by so many white people and the changes that had already taken place—statues of white racists coming down, the Confederate flag burned at NASCAR events, the Mississippi legislature voting to remove the Confederate colors from its state flag, more and more people agreeing that Colin Kaepernick's taking a knee during the National Anthem was a legitimate way to protest police brutality. But the venom exhibited today by the white counter protestors made Sam wonder if the momentum would continue. Even if Biden won in November, the country would probably lapse into the old status quo where racism is not only tolerated but thrives.

"What are you doing out here this time of night, neighbor?"

"Jesus, Doug! You scared the shit out of me."

"Didn't mean to. I thought you saw me coming."

"I was too busy thinking about things I can't do anything about. Normally you and Carol are stacking Zs by now."

"We were about to give it a try when I noticed movement out here. I wanted to make sure it wasn't one of those militia types come back to exact some revenge."

"Yeah, I heard what that guy said to you. Hopefully he was just blowing smoke."

"Probably was. As long as we don't press charges, they'll think they won. After all, they did interrupt the march and that damn monument they care so much about is still standing."

"That's right, but they're the ones ended up turning tail and going home. Thanks to some quick thinking on your part."

"Yeah, well, an old washed-up sheriff has to be good for something."

The two men talked for another ten minutes or so, mostly small talk. Then they fell silent for a while, both watching as the clouds moved past the moon and individual plants in the garden began taking shape.

Sam scanned the vegetation until his eyes came to rest on the small watermelon patch.

"We've got exactly three melons coming," he said, deciding that a little trash talk might be in order. "Don't you think that as a black man I deserve two of 'em?"

"Absolutely not," Doug replied after a pause. "What you deserve, Sam, is equality. And that's exactly what you're going to get, at least from me. We're going to split that third melon right down the middle."

Sam chuckled. "Fair enough, brother," he said. "But I want to be the one doin' the cuttin'."